BABY-SITTERS LITTLE SISTER®

KAREN'S KITTYCAT CLUB

**DON'T MISS THE OTHER BABY-SITTERS
LITTLE SISTER GRAPHIC NOVELS!**

KAREN'S WITCH

KAREN'S ROLLER SKATES

KAREN'S WORST DAY

ANN M. MARTIN
BABY-SITTERS LITTLE SISTER®

KAREN'S KITTYCAT CLUB

A GRAPHIC NOVEL BY

KATY FARINA

WITH COLOR BY BRADEN LAMB

graphix

An Imprint of

SCHOLASTIC

Library of Congress Control Number: 2020943059

ISBN 978-1-338-35622-9 (hardcover)
ISBN 978-1-338-35621-2 (paperback)

10 9 8 7 6 5 4 3 2 1   21 22 23 24 25

Printed in China   62
First edition, July 2021

Edited by Cassandra Pelham Fulton and David Levithan
Book design by Shivana Sookdeo
Creative Director: Phil Falco
Publisher: David Saylor

For Jennifer Esty, a big sister
A. M. M.

For my cats, Poe and Guinness, and to
every animal that warms our hearts
K. F.

CHAPTER 1

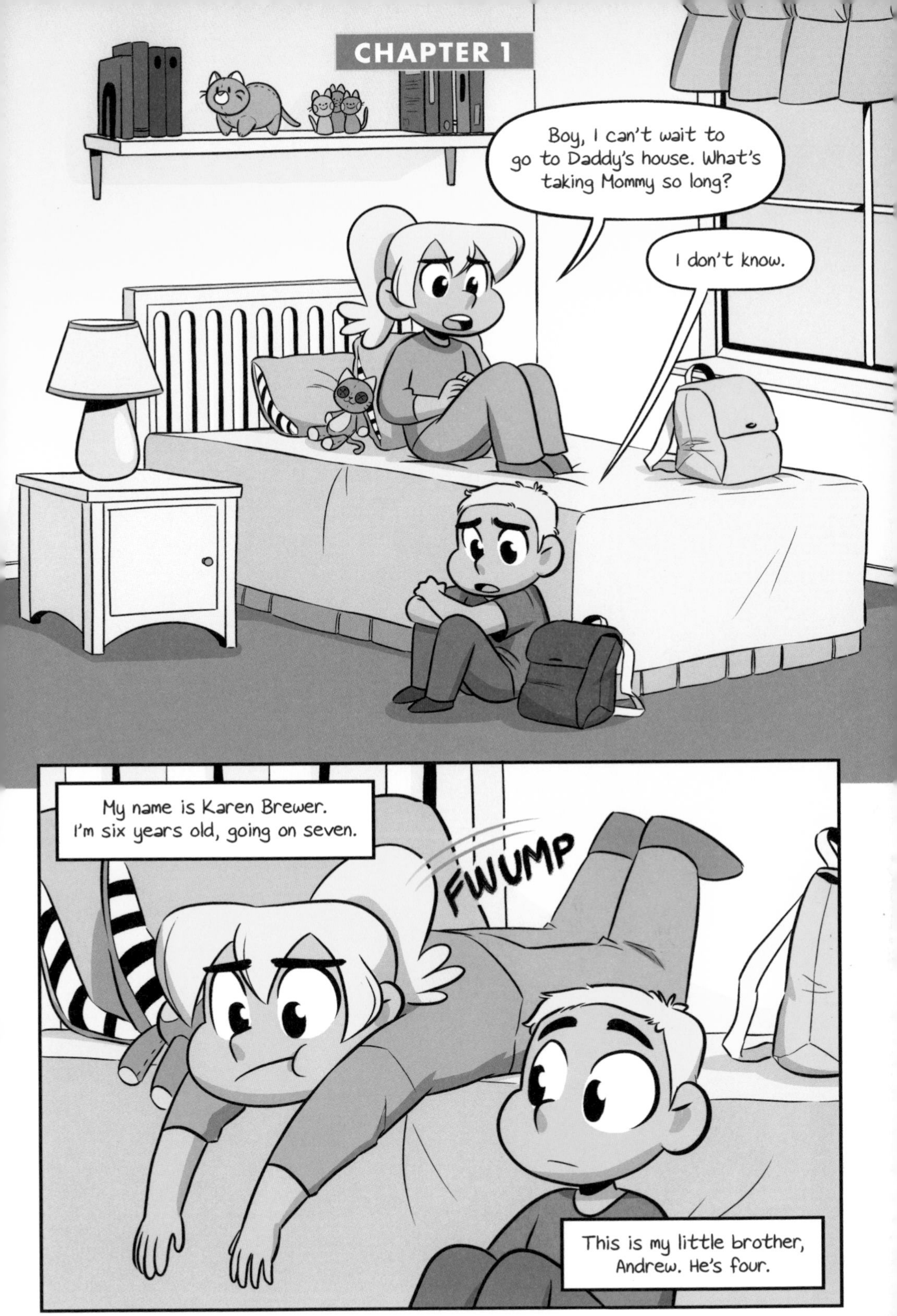
Boy, I can't wait to go to Daddy's house. What's taking Mommy so long?
I don't know.
My name is Karen Brewer. I'm six years old, going on seven.
FWUMP
This is my little brother, Andrew. He's four.

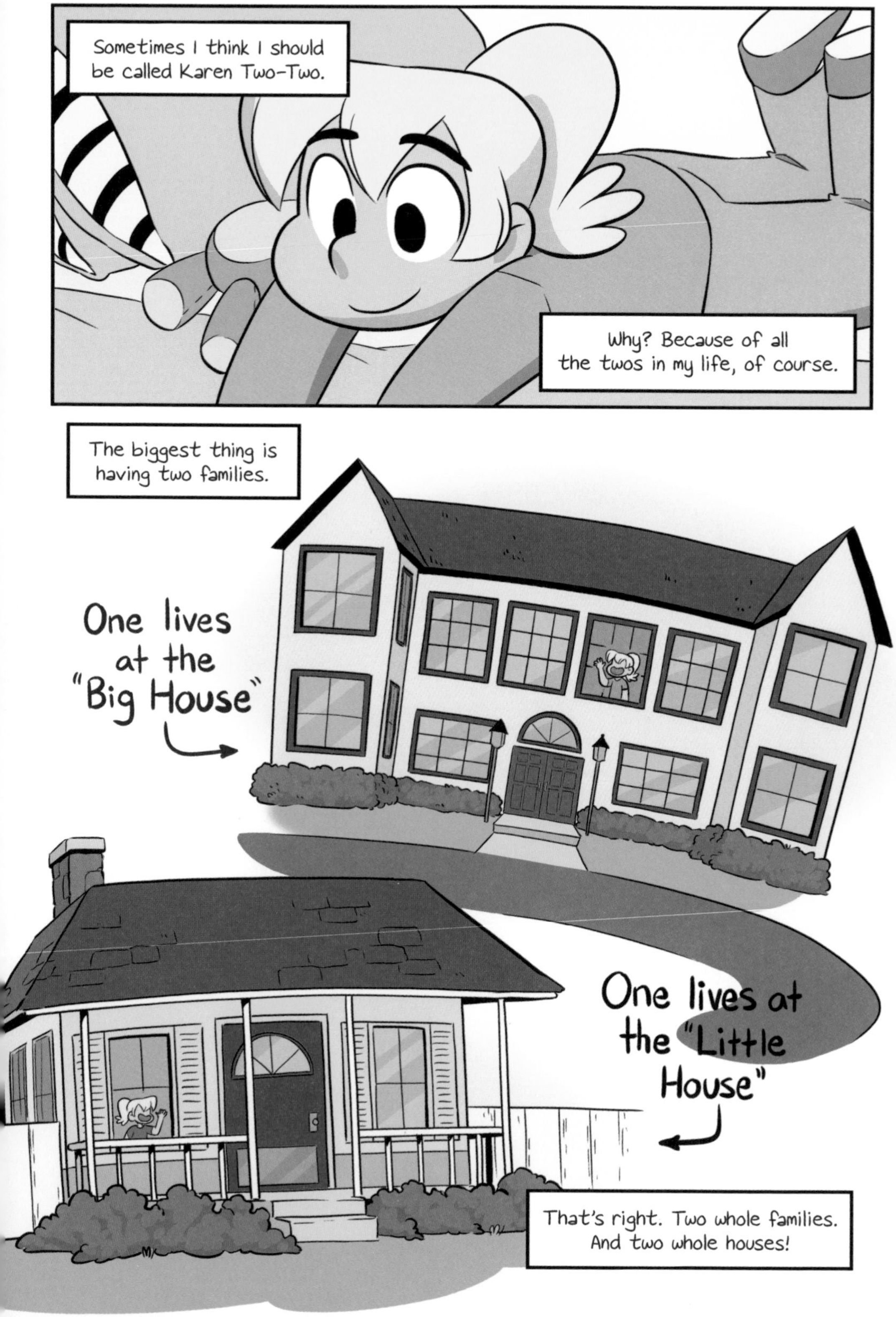
Sometimes I think I should be called Karen Two-Two.
Why? Because of all the twos in my life, of course.
The biggest thing is having two families.
One lives at the "Big House"
One lives at the "Little House"
That's right. Two whole families. And two whole houses!

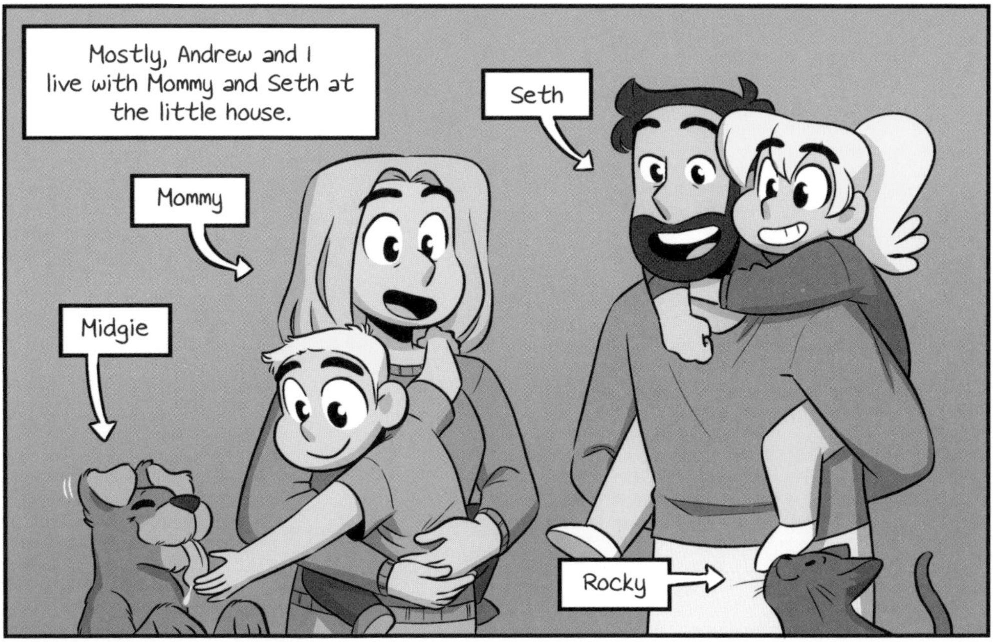
Mostly, Andrew and I live with Mommy and Seth at the little house.
Seth
Mommy
Midgie
Rocky

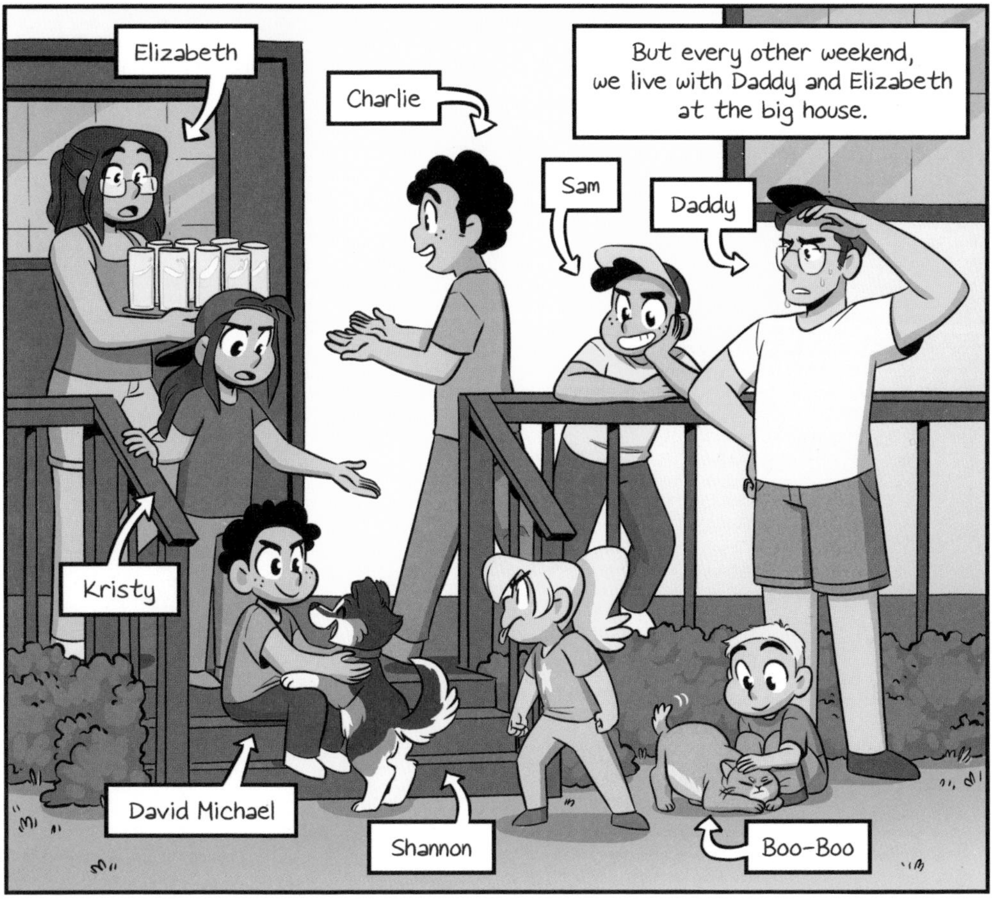
Elizabeth
Charlie
But every other weekend, we live with Daddy and Elizabeth at the big house.
Sam
Daddy
Kristy
David Michael
Shannon
Boo-Boo

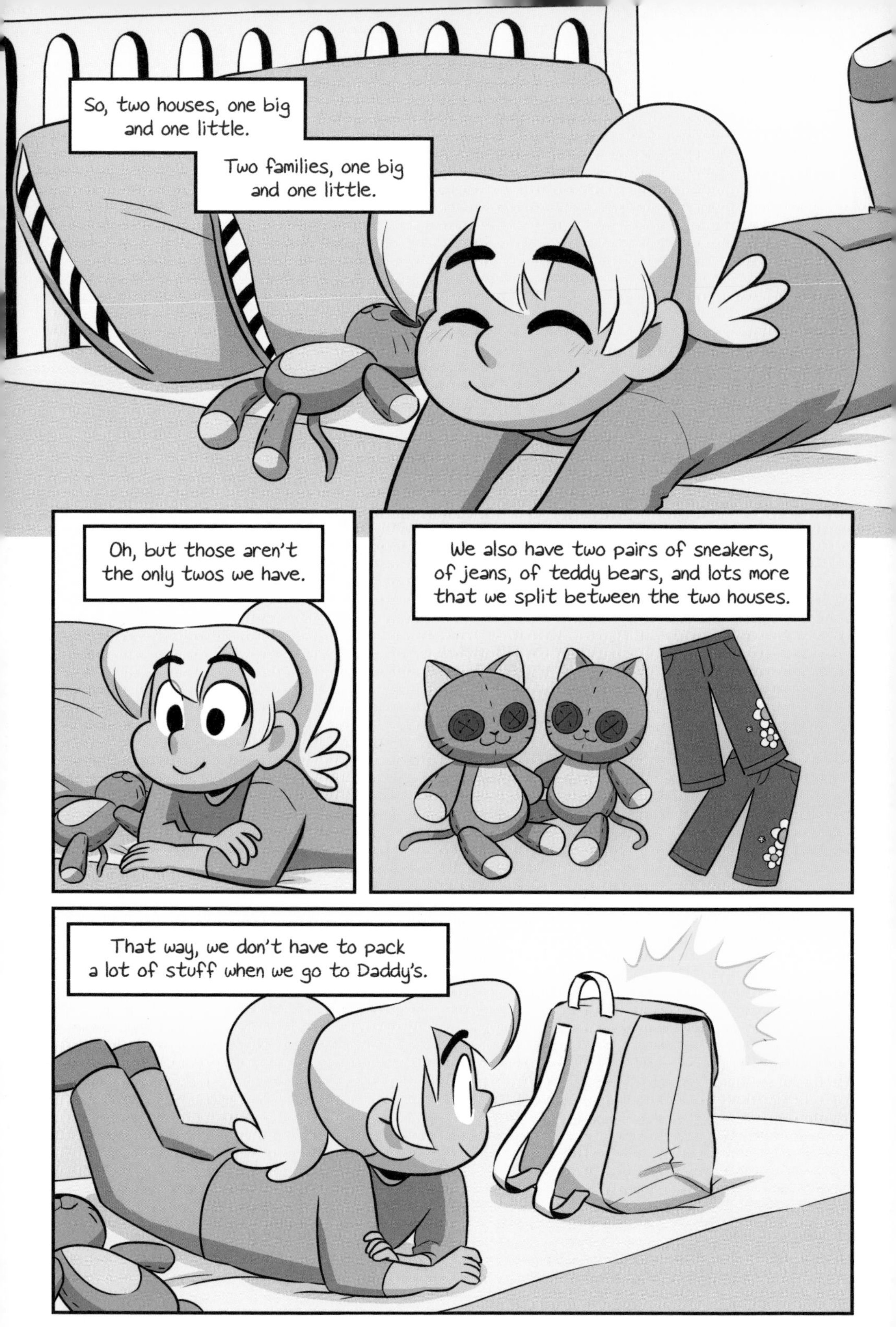
So, two houses, one big and one little.
Two families, one big and one little.
Oh, but those aren't the only twos we have.
We also have two pairs of sneakers, of jeans, of teddy bears, and lots more that we split between the two houses.
That way, we don't have to pack a lot of stuff when we go to Daddy's.

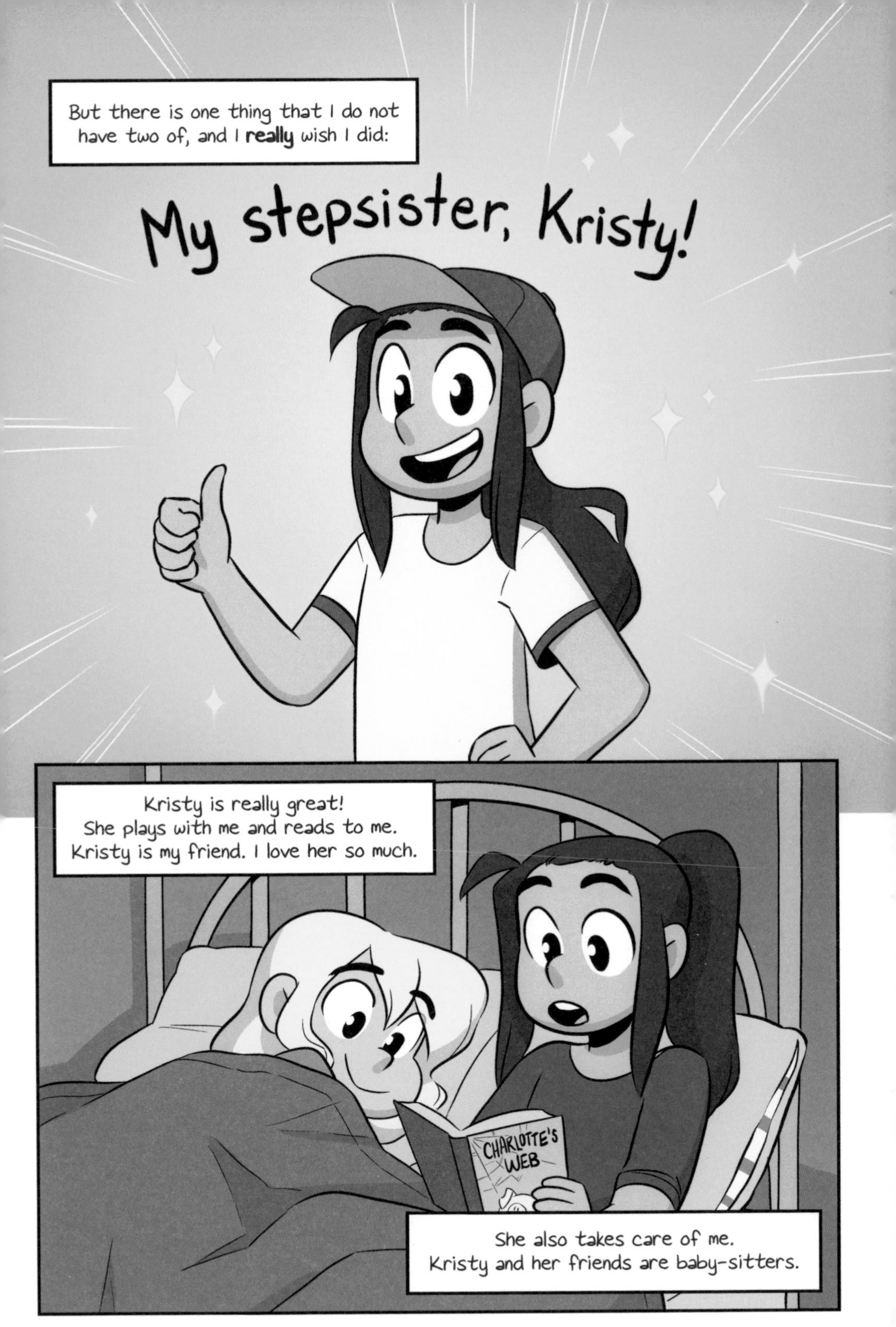
But there is one thing that I do not have two of, and I **really** wish I did:
My stepsister, Kristy!
Kristy is really great!
She plays with me and reads to me.
Kristy is my friend. I love her so much.
CHARLOTTE'S WEB
She also takes care of me.
Kristy and her friends are baby-sitters.

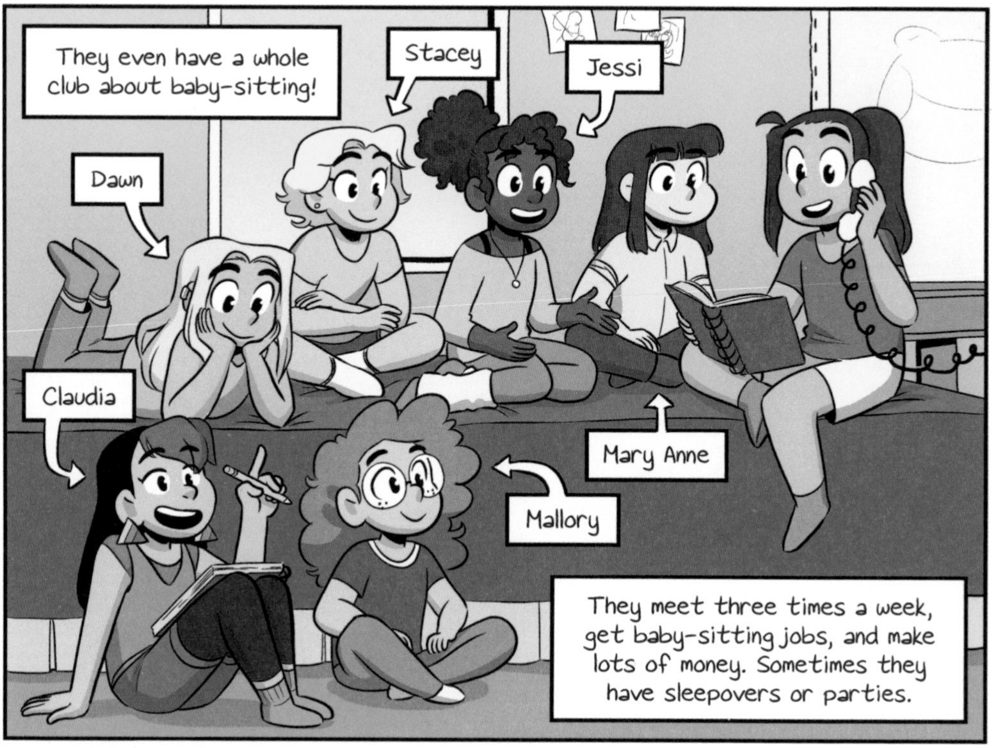
They even have a whole club about baby-sitting!
Stacey
Jessi
Dawn
Claudia
Mary Anne
Mallory
They meet three times a week, get baby-sitting jobs, and make lots of money. Sometimes they have sleepovers or parties.

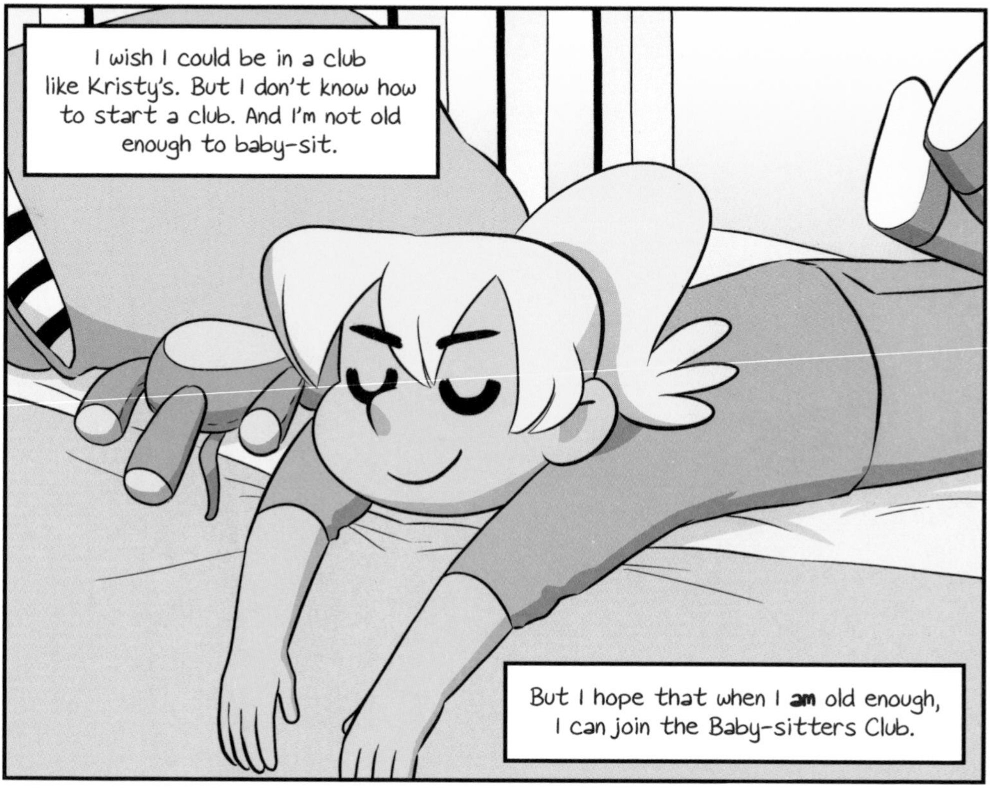
I wish I could be in a club like Kristy's. But I don't know how to start a club. And I'm not old enough to baby-sit.
But I hope that when I **am** old enough, I can join the Baby-sitters Club.

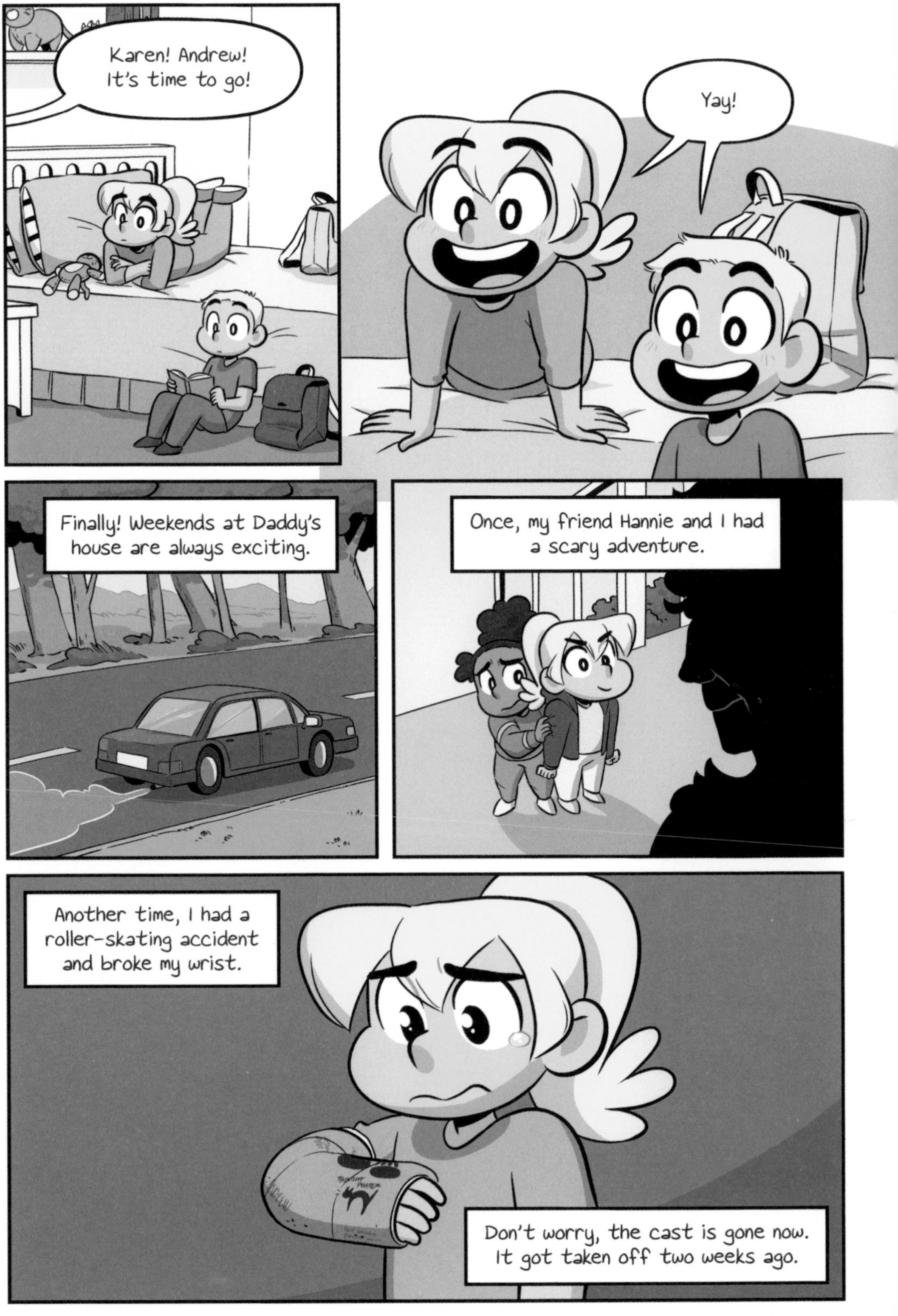
Karen! Andrew! It's time to go!
Yay!
Finally! Weekends at Daddy's house are always exciting.
Once, my friend Hannie and I had a scary adventure.
Another time, I had a roller-skating accident and broke my wrist.
Don't worry, the cast is gone now. It got taken off two weeks ago.

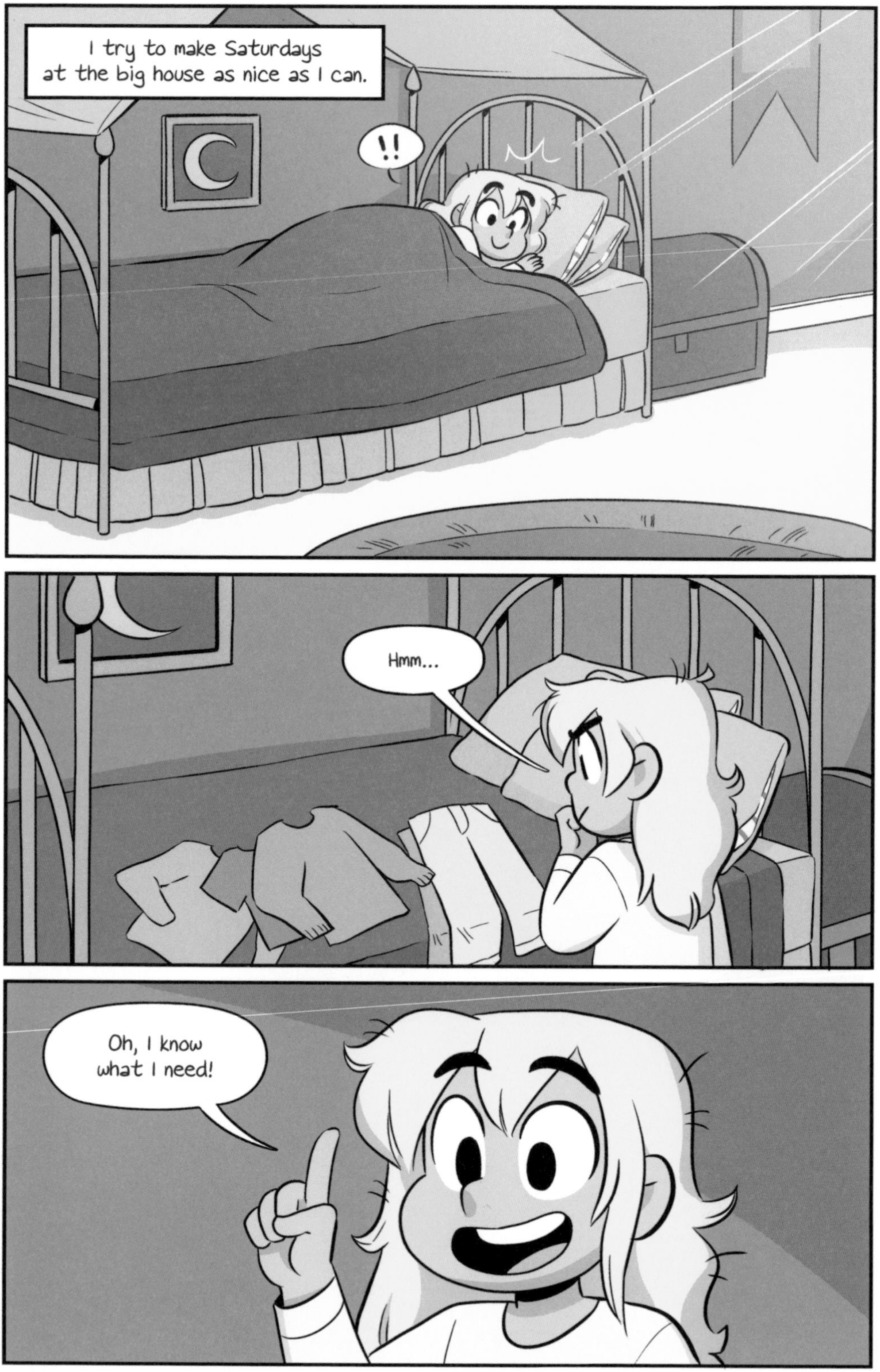
I try to make Saturdays at the big house as nice as I can.
!!
Hmm...
Oh, I know what I need!

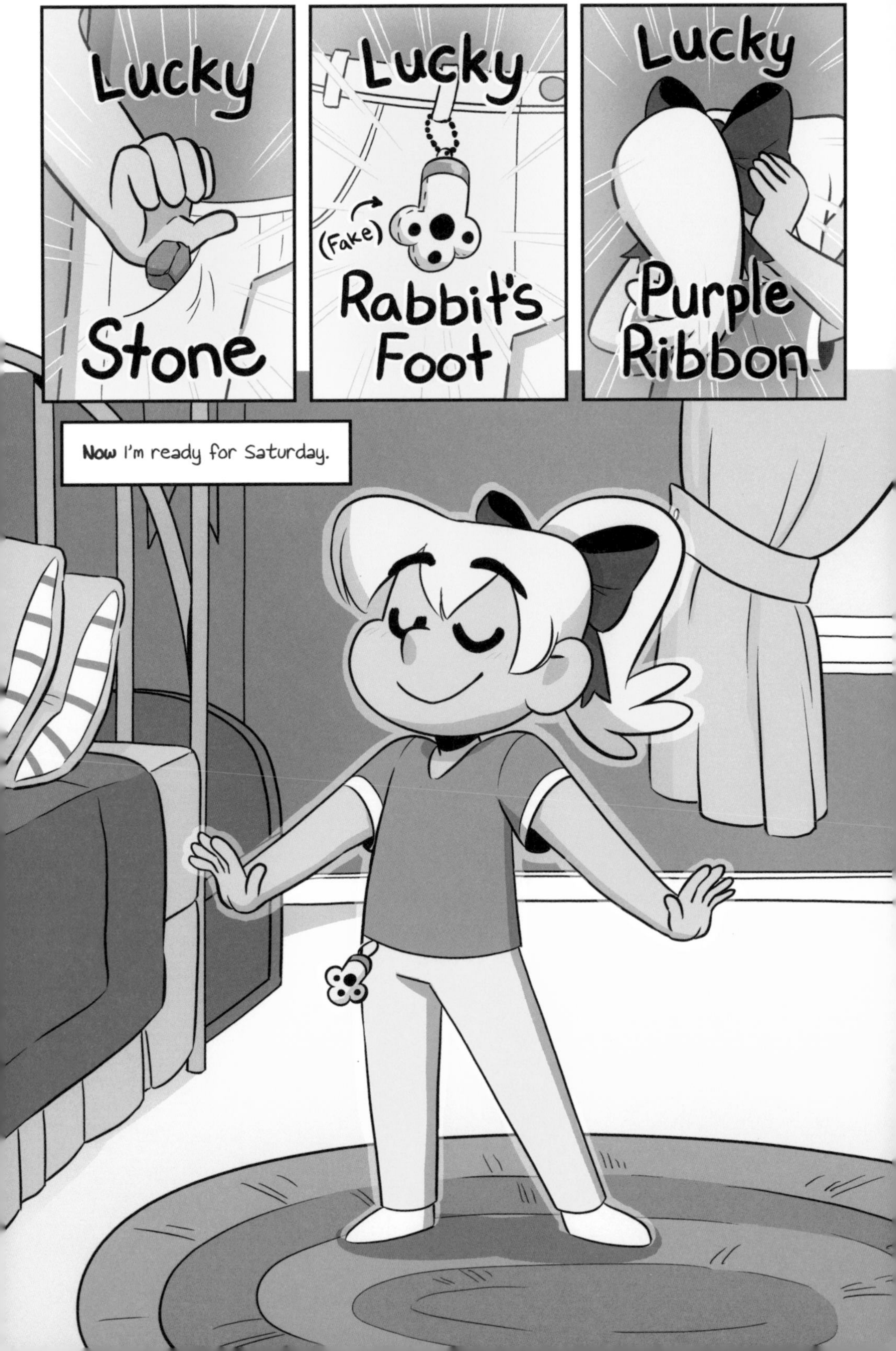
Lucky
Stone
Lucky
(Fake)
Rabbit's
Foot
Lucky
Purple
Ribbon
Now I'm ready for Saturday.

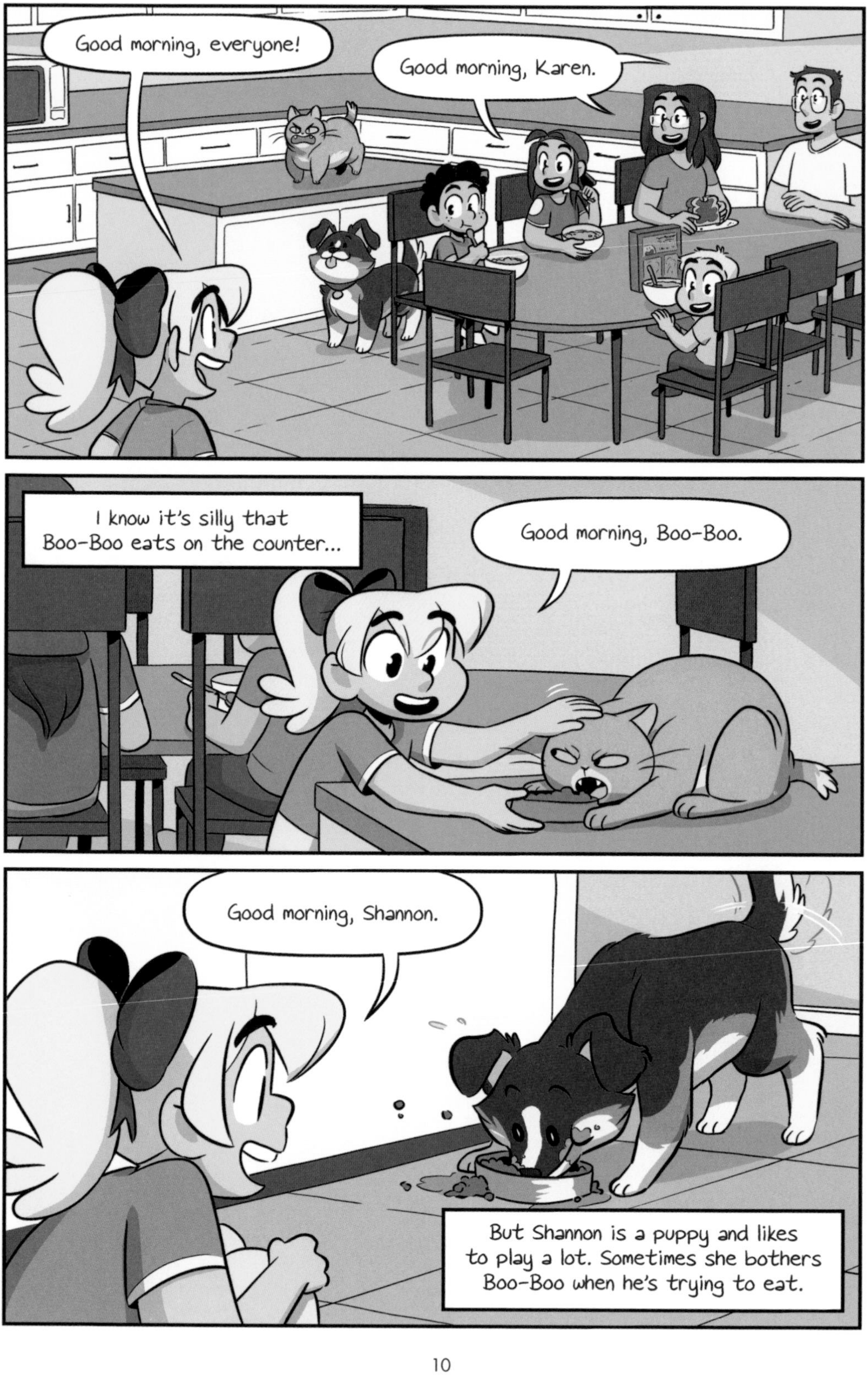
Good morning, everyone!
Good morning, Karen.
I know it's silly that Boo-Boo eats on the counter...
Good morning, Boo-Boo.
Good morning, Shannon.
But Shannon is a puppy and likes to play a lot. Sometimes she bothers Boo-Boo when he's trying to eat.

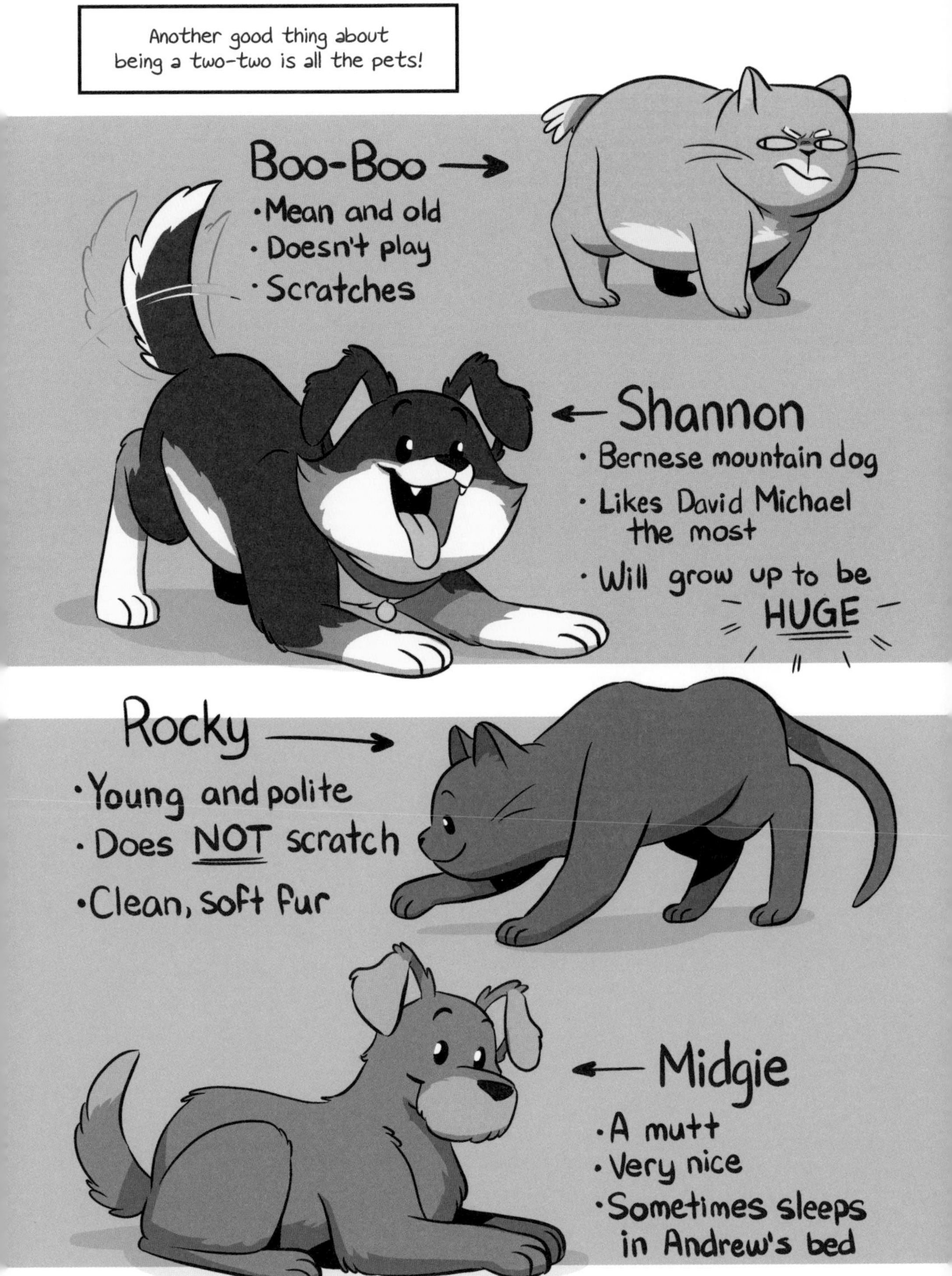
Another good thing about being a two-two is all the pets!
Boo-Boo
•Mean and old
•Doesn't play
•Scratches
Shannon
•Bernese mountain dog
•Likes David Michael the most
•Will grow up to be HUGE
Rocky
•Young and polite
•Does NOT scratch
•Clean, soft fur
Midgie
•A mutt
•Very nice
•Sometimes sleeps in Andrew's bed

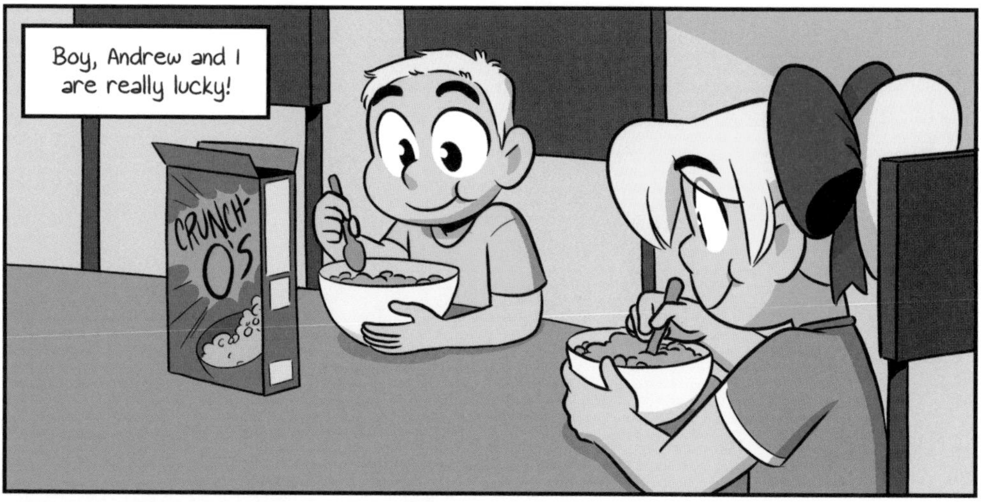
Boy, Andrew and I are really lucky!
CRUNCH-O'S

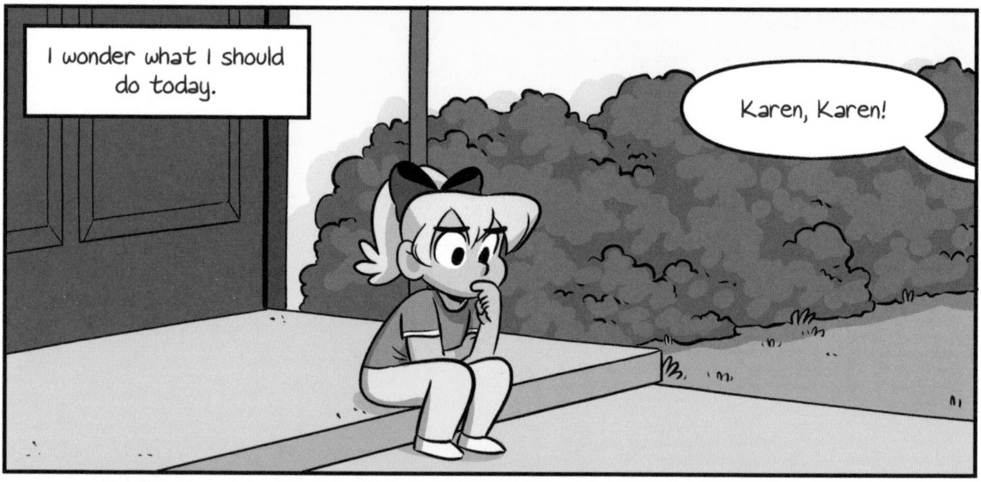
I wonder what I should do today.
Karen, Karen!

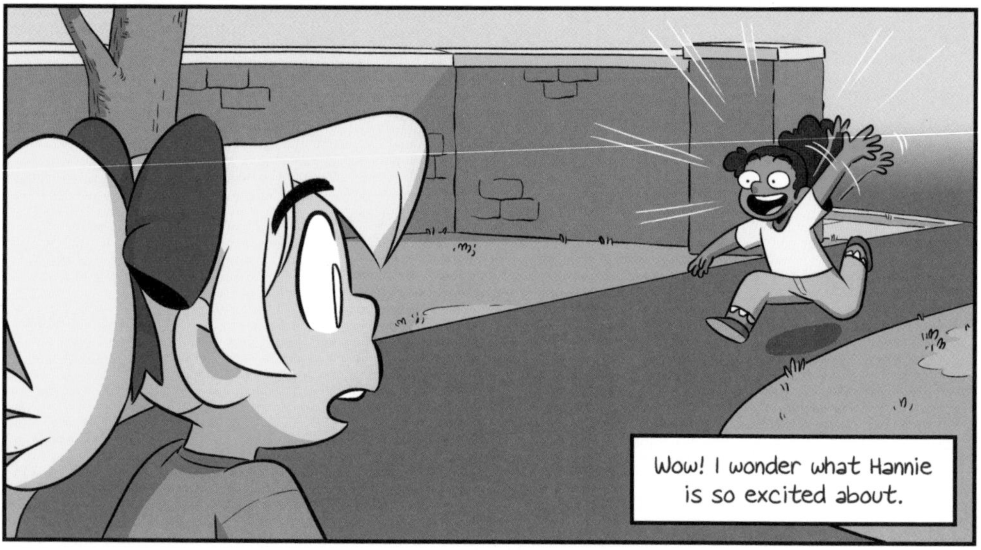
Wow! I wonder what Hannie is so excited about.

CHAPTER 2

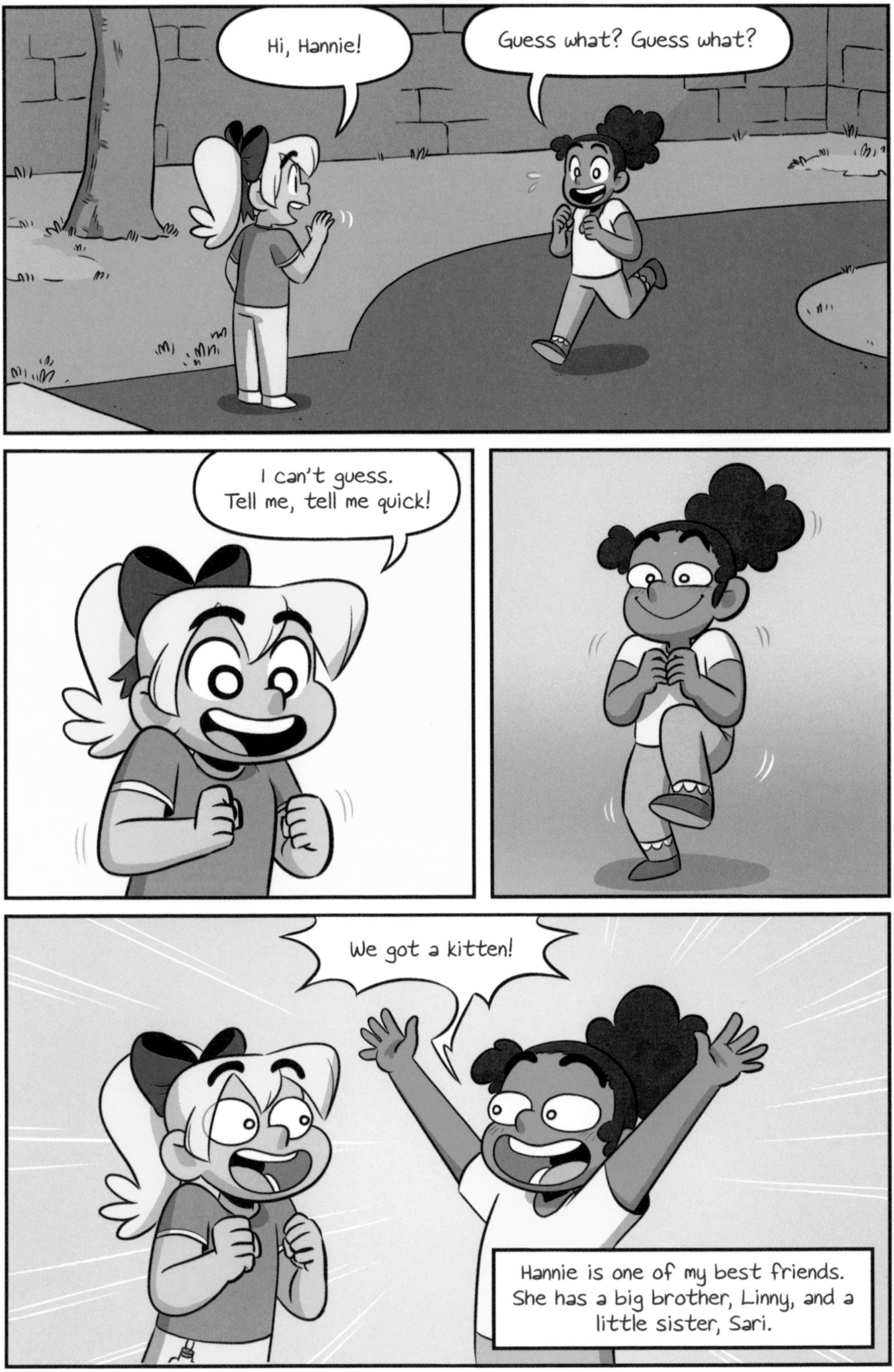

Hi, Hannie!
Guess what? Guess what?
I can't guess. Tell me, tell me quick!
We got a kitten!
Hannie is one of my best friends. She has a big brother, Linny, and a little sister, Sari.

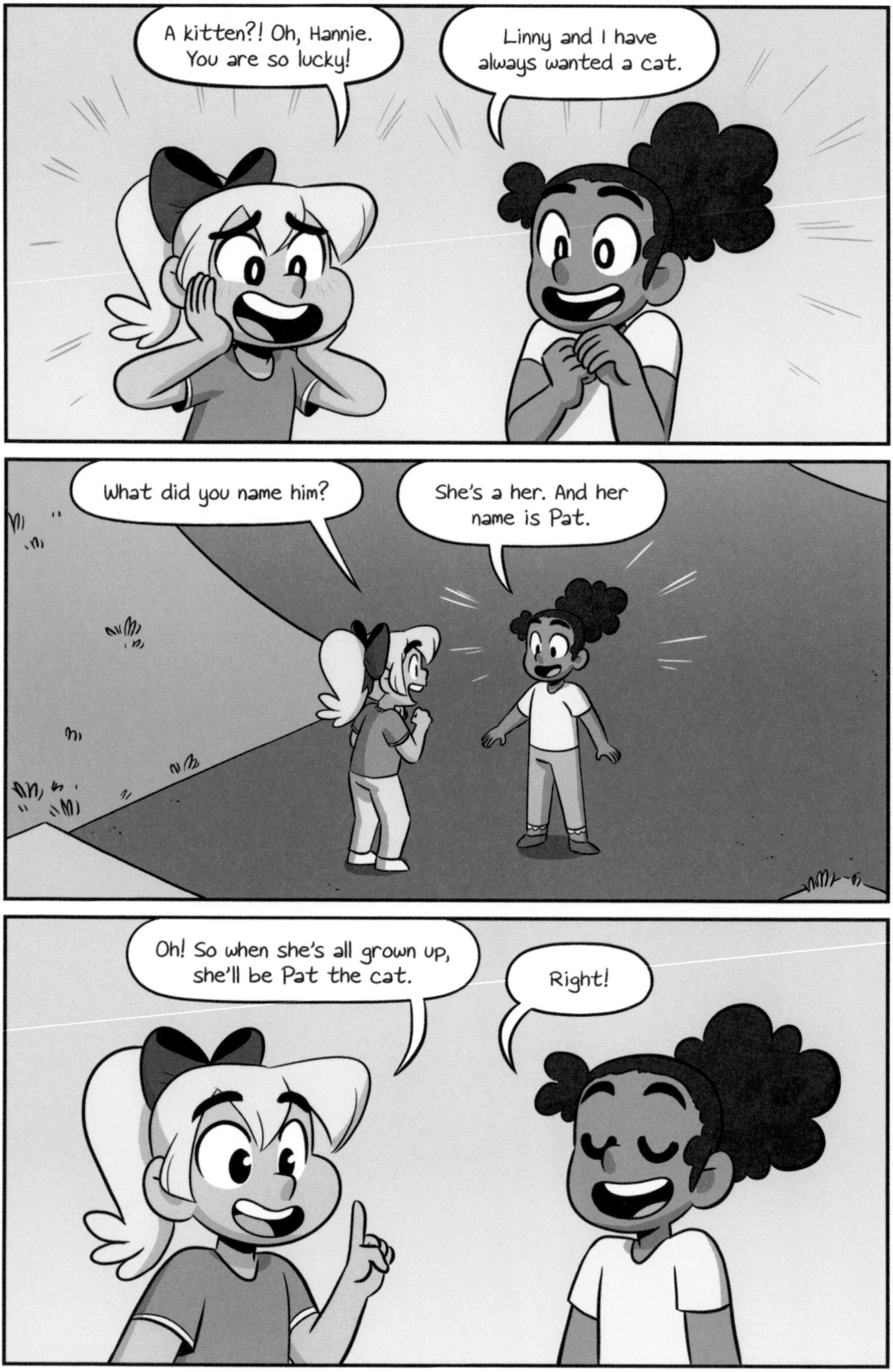
A kitten?! Oh, Hannie. You are so lucky!
Linny and I have always wanted a cat.
What did you name him?
She's a her. And her name is Pat.
Oh! So when she's all grown up, she'll be Pat the cat.
Right!

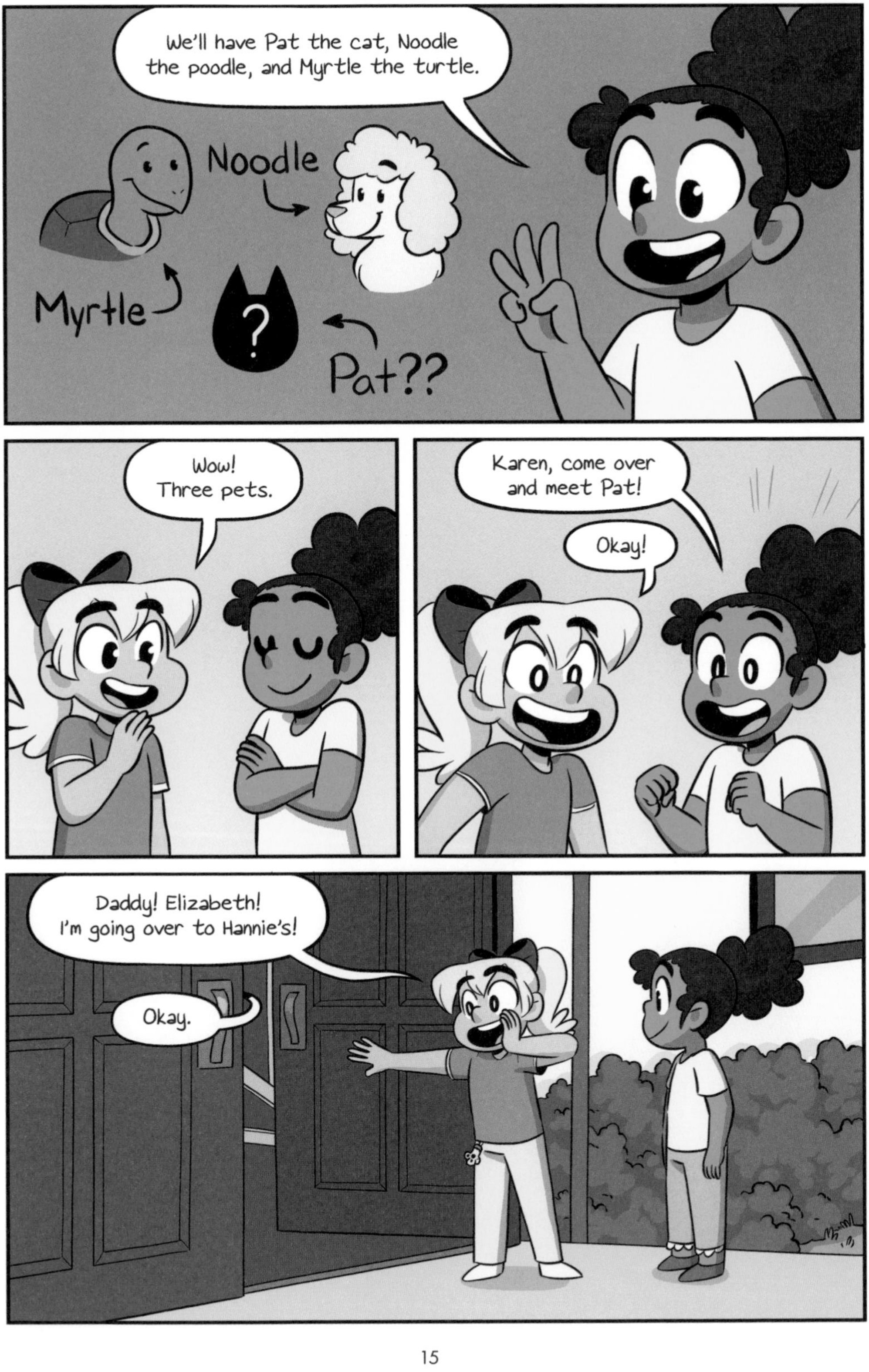
We'll have Pat the cat, Noodle the poodle, and Myrtle the turtle.
Noodle
Myrtle
?
Pat??
Wow! Three pets.
Karen, come over and meet Pat!
Okay!
Daddy! Elizabeth! I'm going over to Hannie's!
Okay.

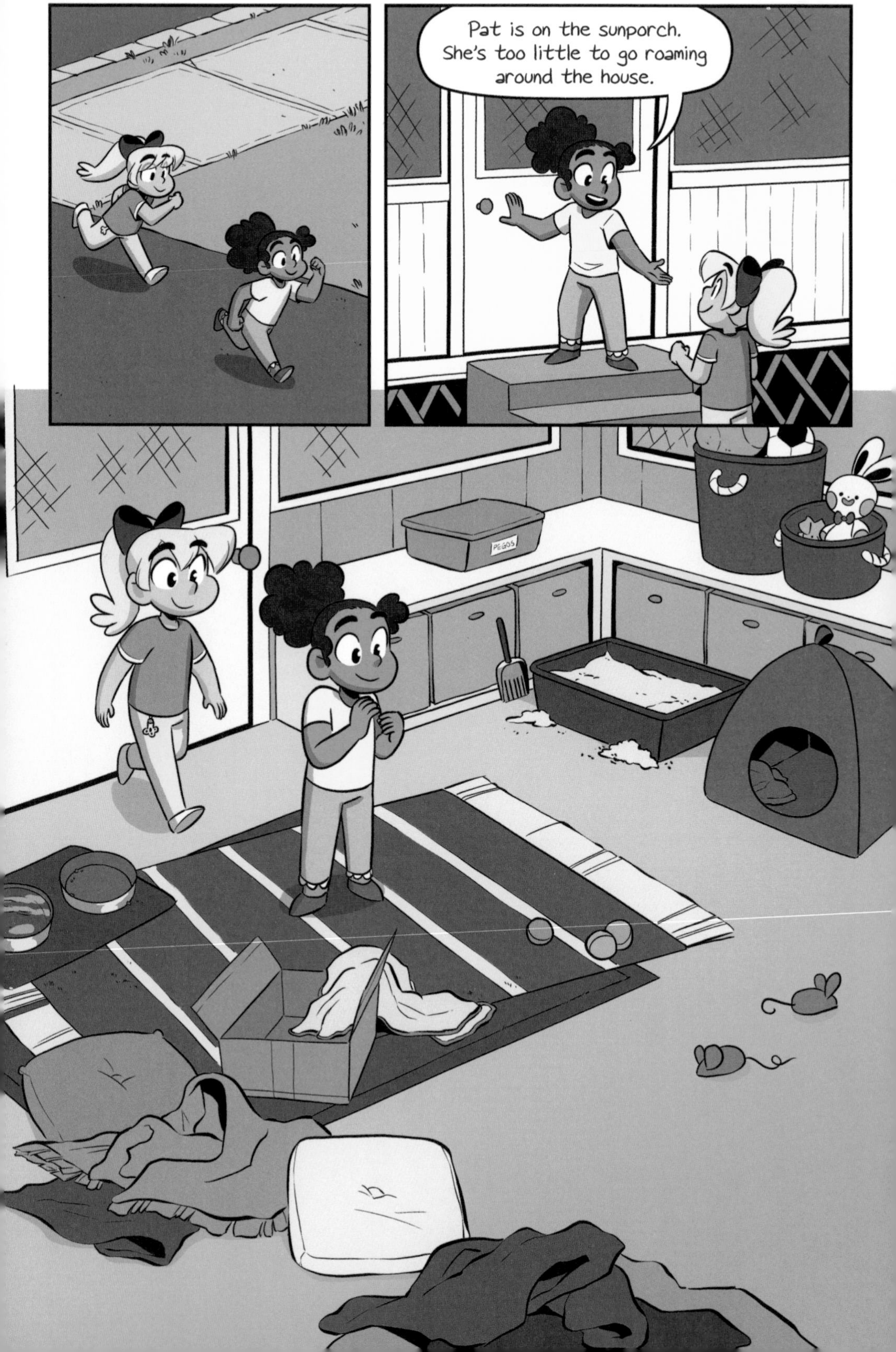
Pat is on the sunporch. She's too little to go roaming around the house.
PEGOS

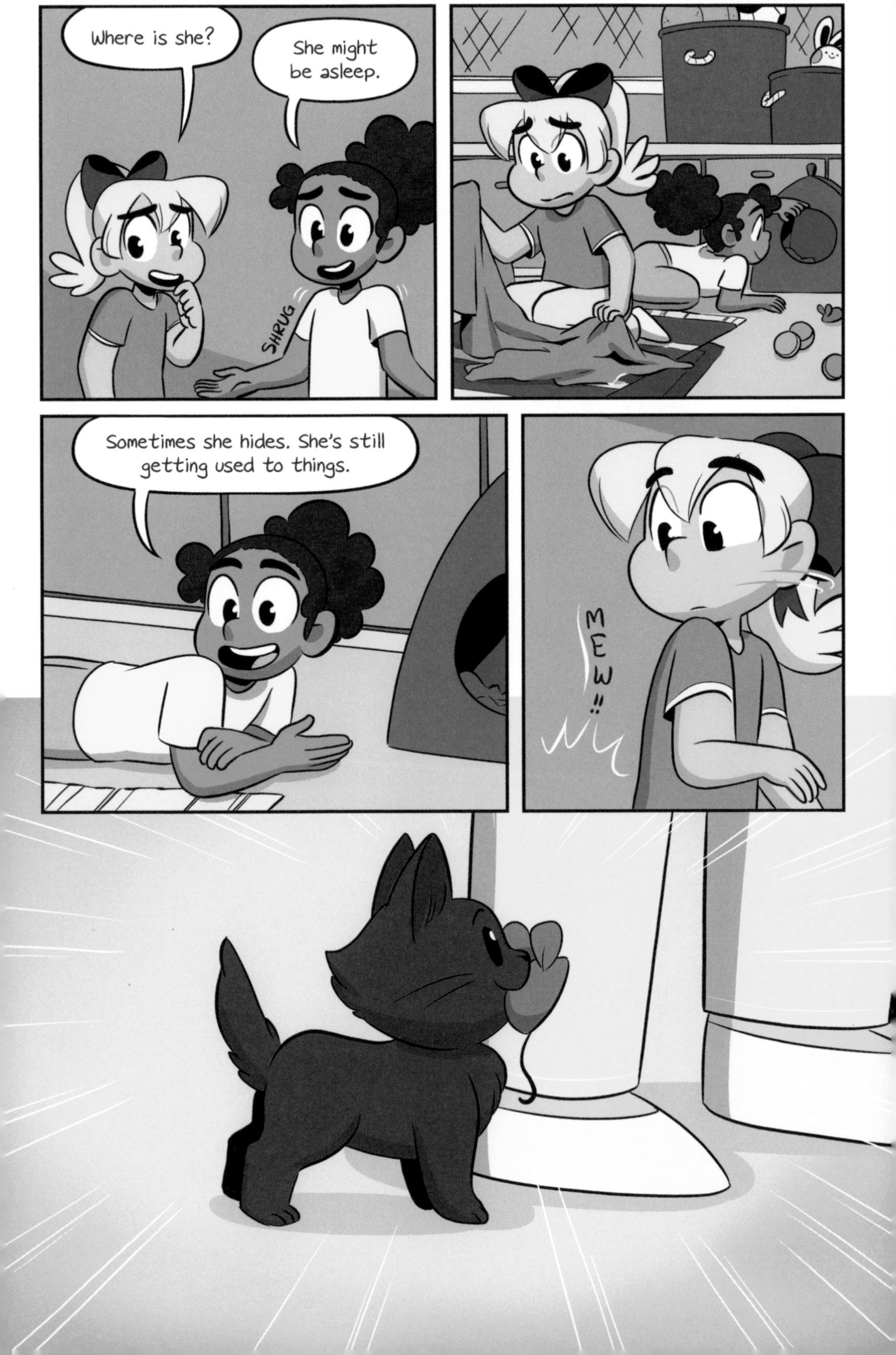
Where is she?
She might be asleep.
SHRUG
Sometimes she hides. She's still getting used to things.
MEW!!

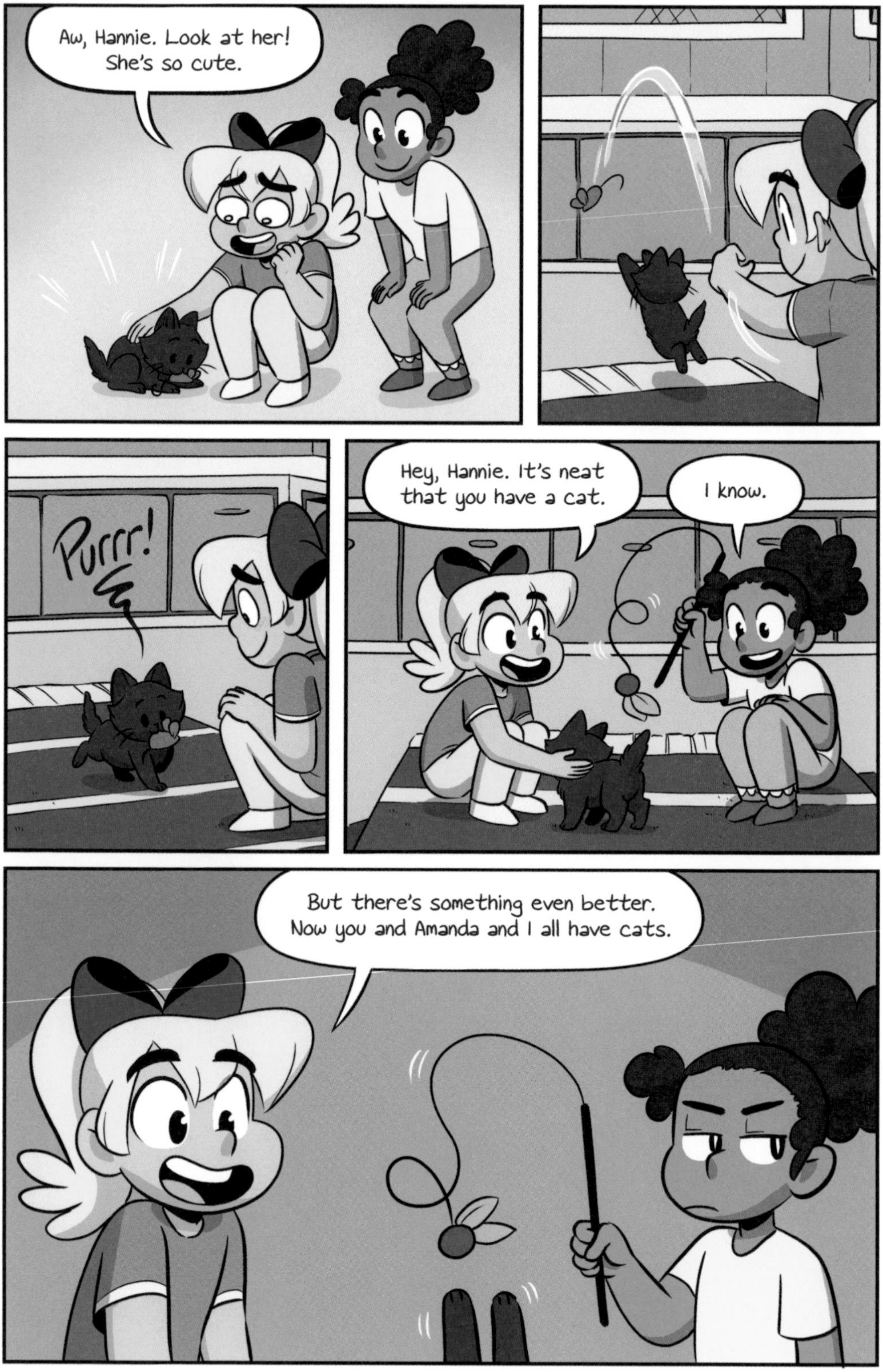
Aw, Hannie. Look at her! She's so cute.
Purrr!
Hey, Hannie. It's neat that you have a cat.
I know.
But there's something even better. Now you and Amanda and I all have cats.

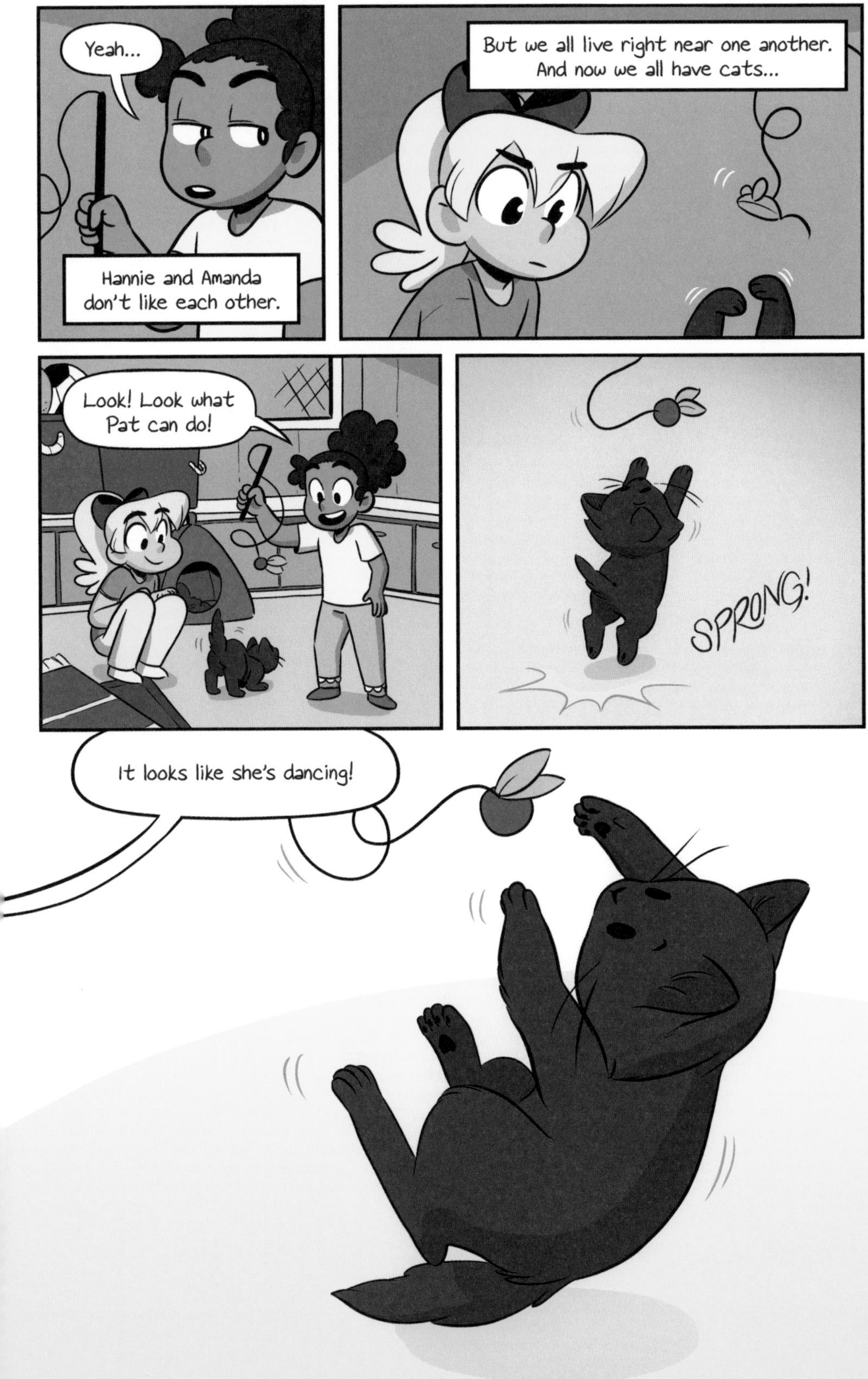
Yeah...
Hannie and Amanda don't like each other.
But we all live right near one another. And now we all have cats...
Look! Look what Pat can do!
SPRONG!
It looks like she's dancing!

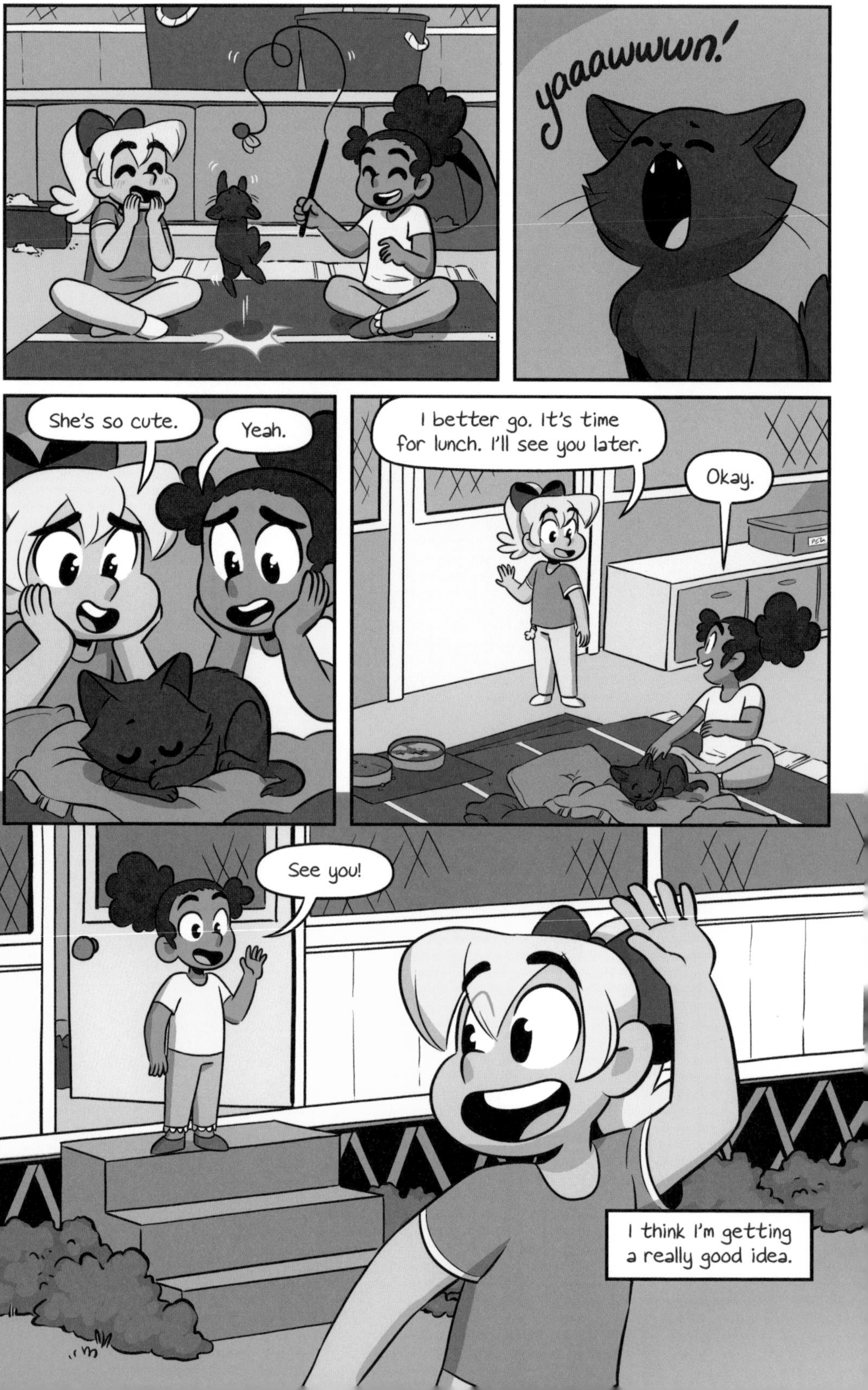
yaaawwwn!
She's so cute.
Yeah.
I better go. It's time for lunch. I'll see you later.
Okay.
See you!
I think I'm getting a really good idea.

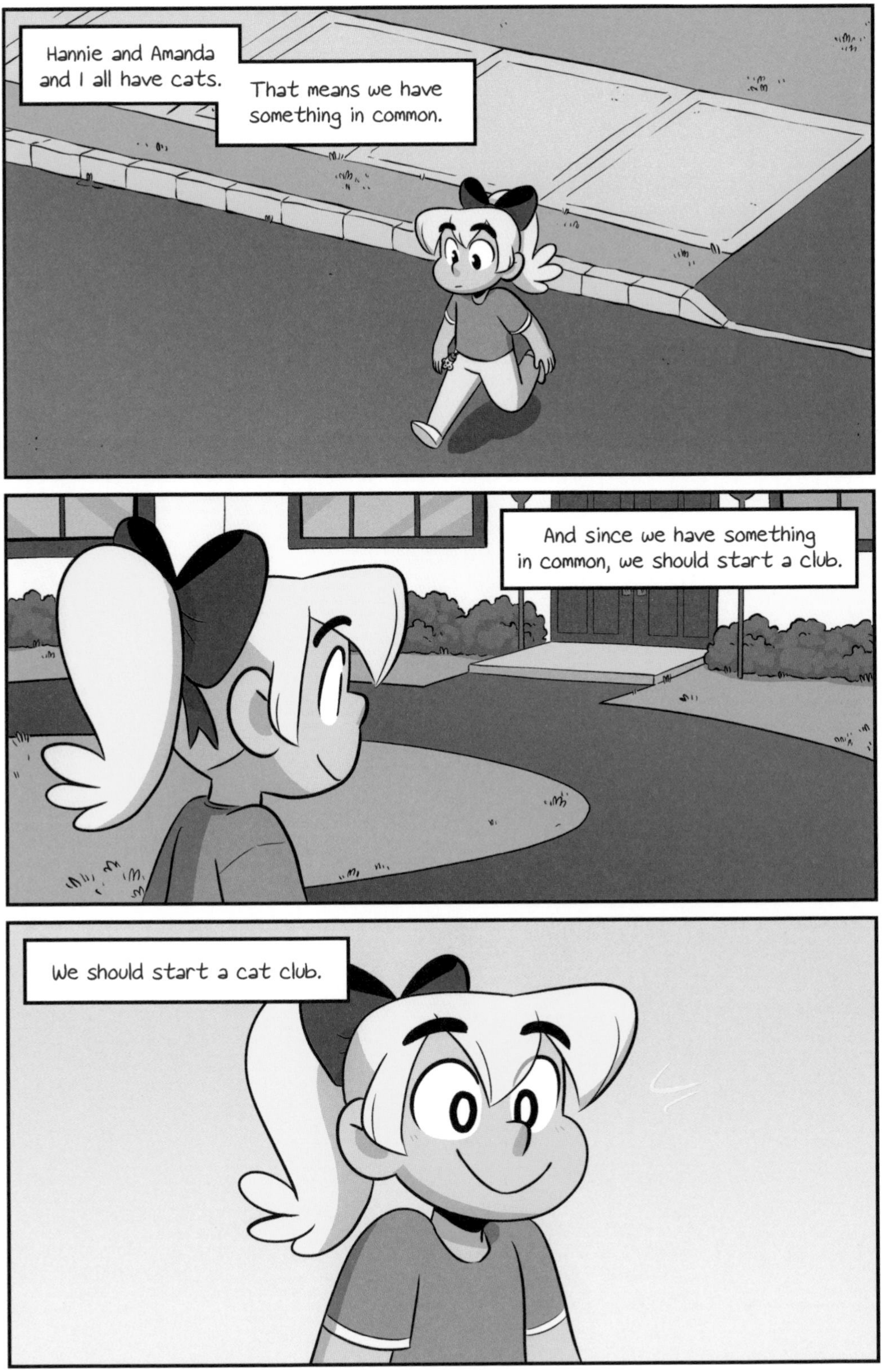
Hannie and Amanda and I all have cats.
That means we have something in common.
And since we have something in common, we should start a club.
We should start a cat club.

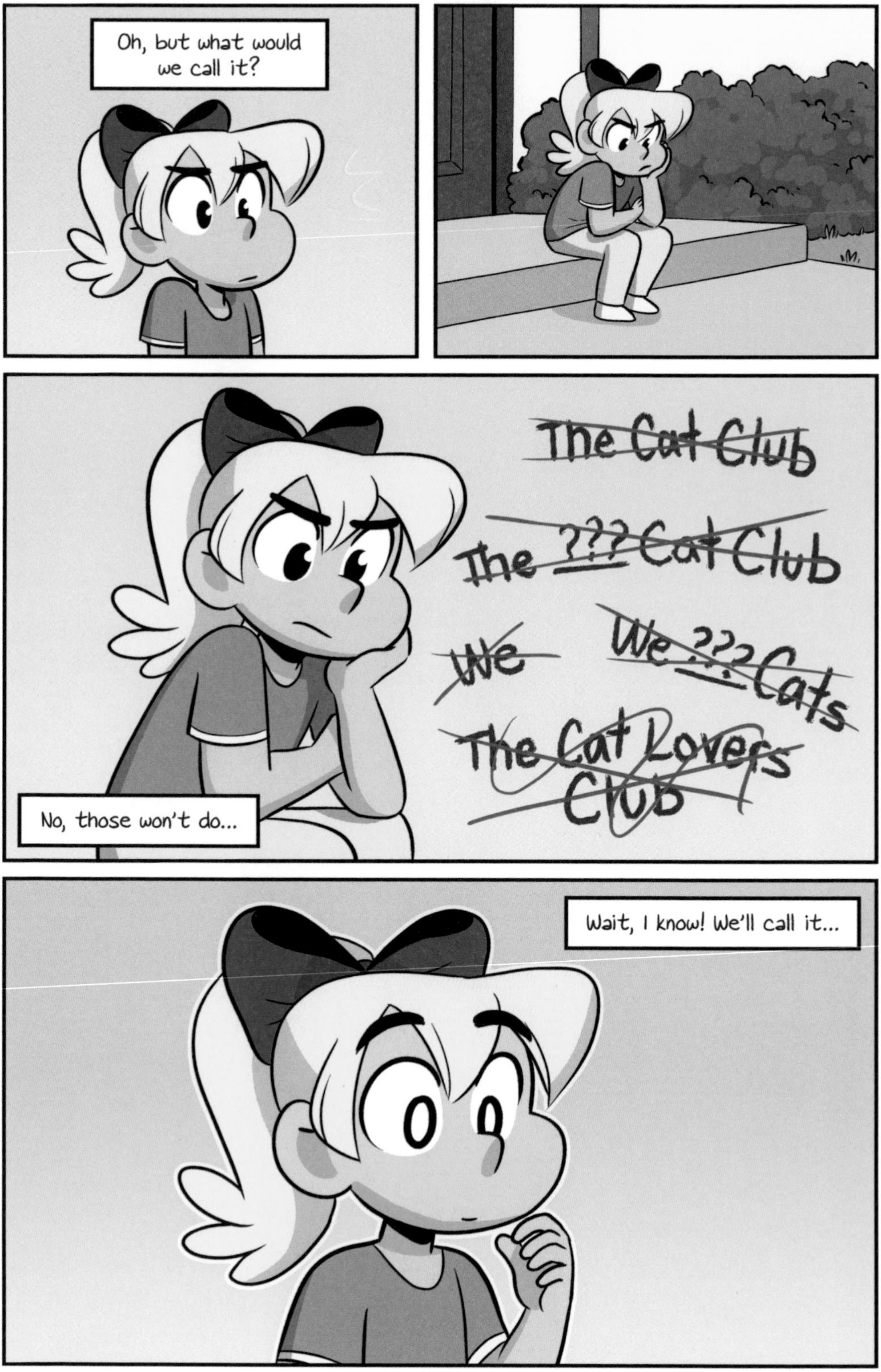
Oh, but what would we call it?
The Cat Club
The ??? Cat Club
We
We ??? Cats
The Cat Lovers Club
No, those won't do...
Wait, I know! We'll call it...

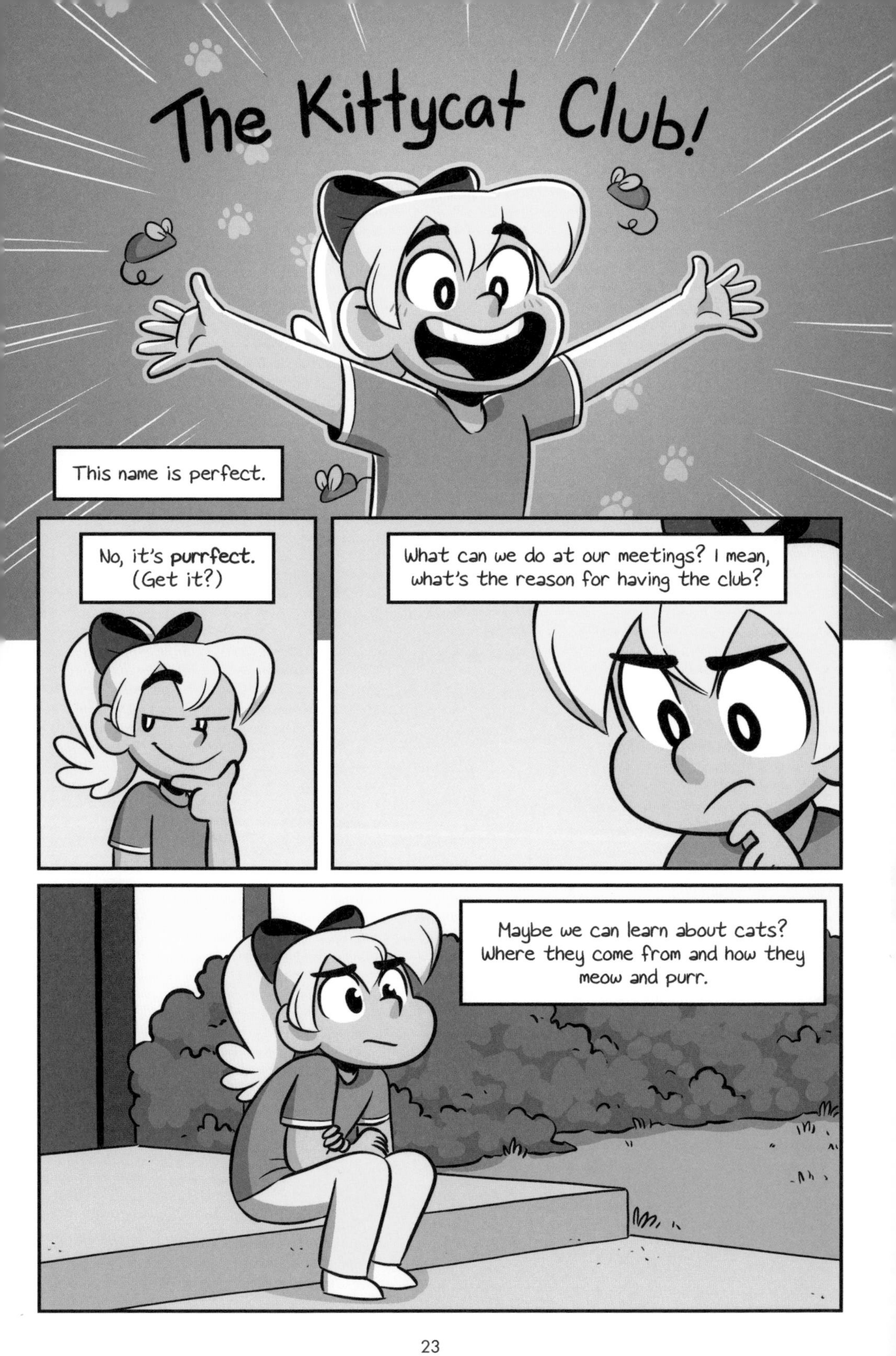
The Kittycat Club!
This name is perfect.
No, it's purrfect. (Get it?)
What can we do at our meetings? I mean, what's the reason for having the club?
Maybe we can learn about cats? Where they come from and how they meow and purr.

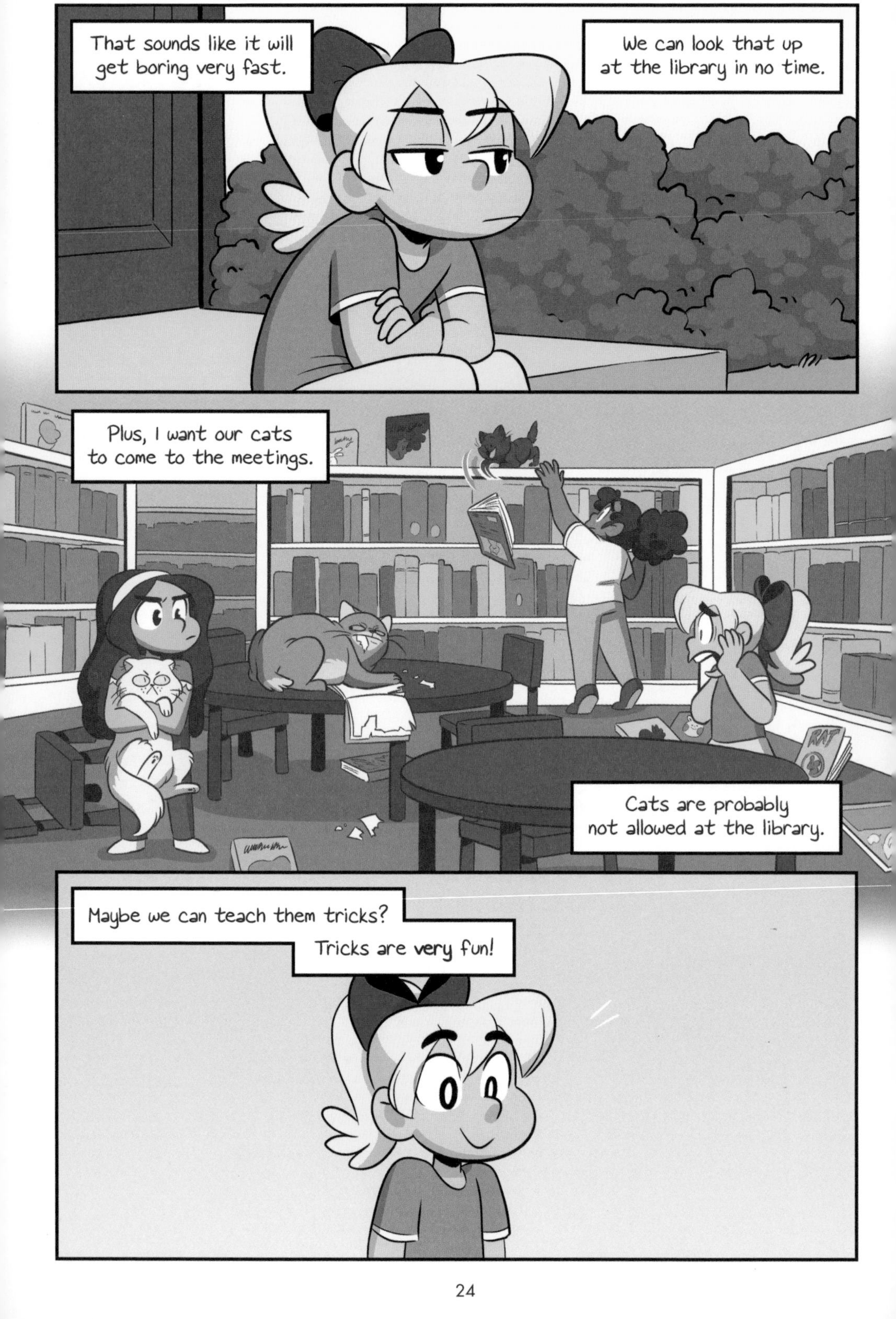
That sounds like it will get boring very fast.
We can look that up at the library in no time.
Plus, I want our cats to come to the meetings.
RAT
Cats are probably not allowed at the library.
Maybe we can teach them tricks?
Tricks are very fun!

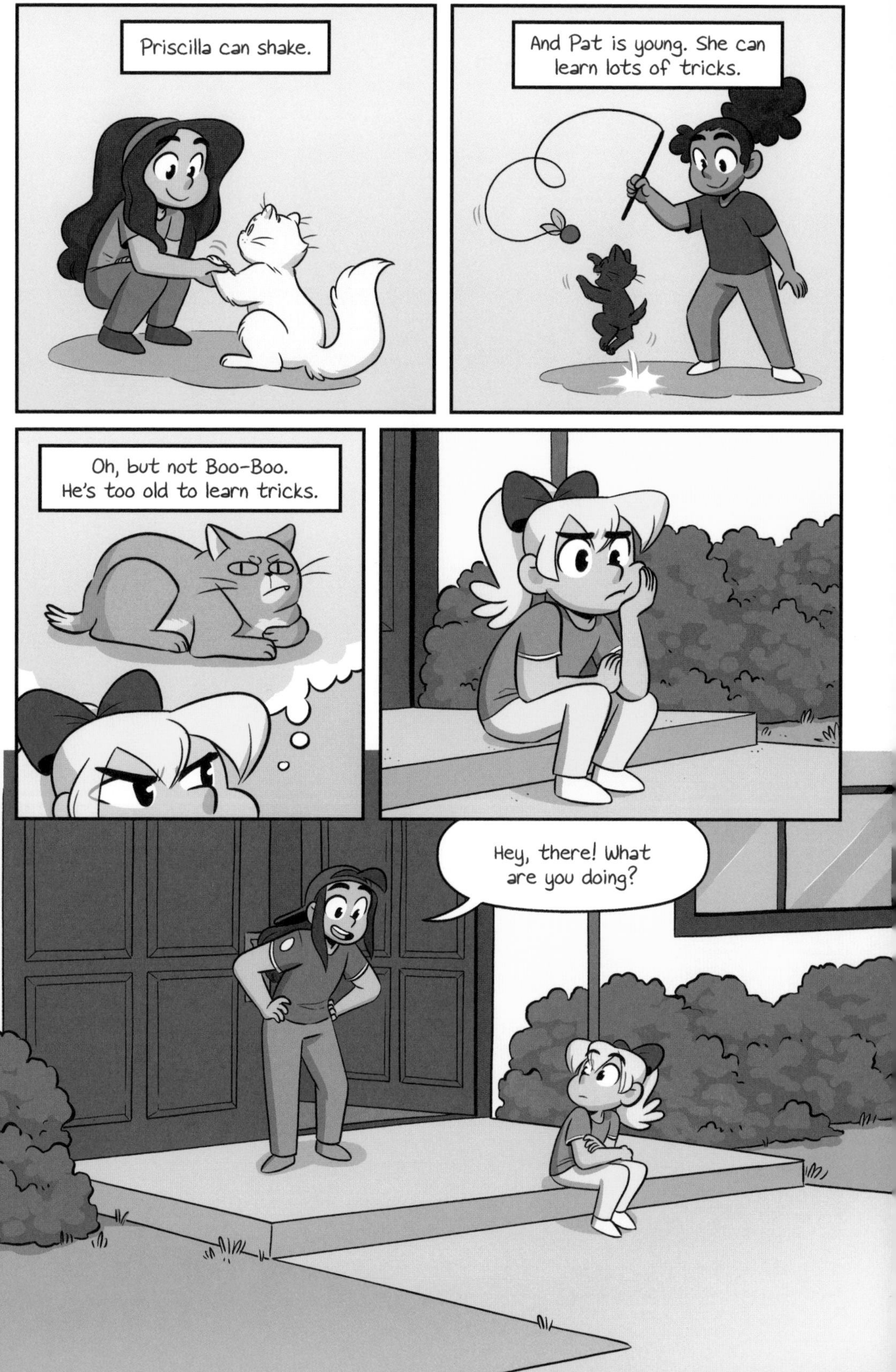
Priscilla can shake.
And Pat is young. She can learn lots of tricks.
Oh, but not Boo-Boo. He's too old to learn tricks.
Hey, there! What are you doing?

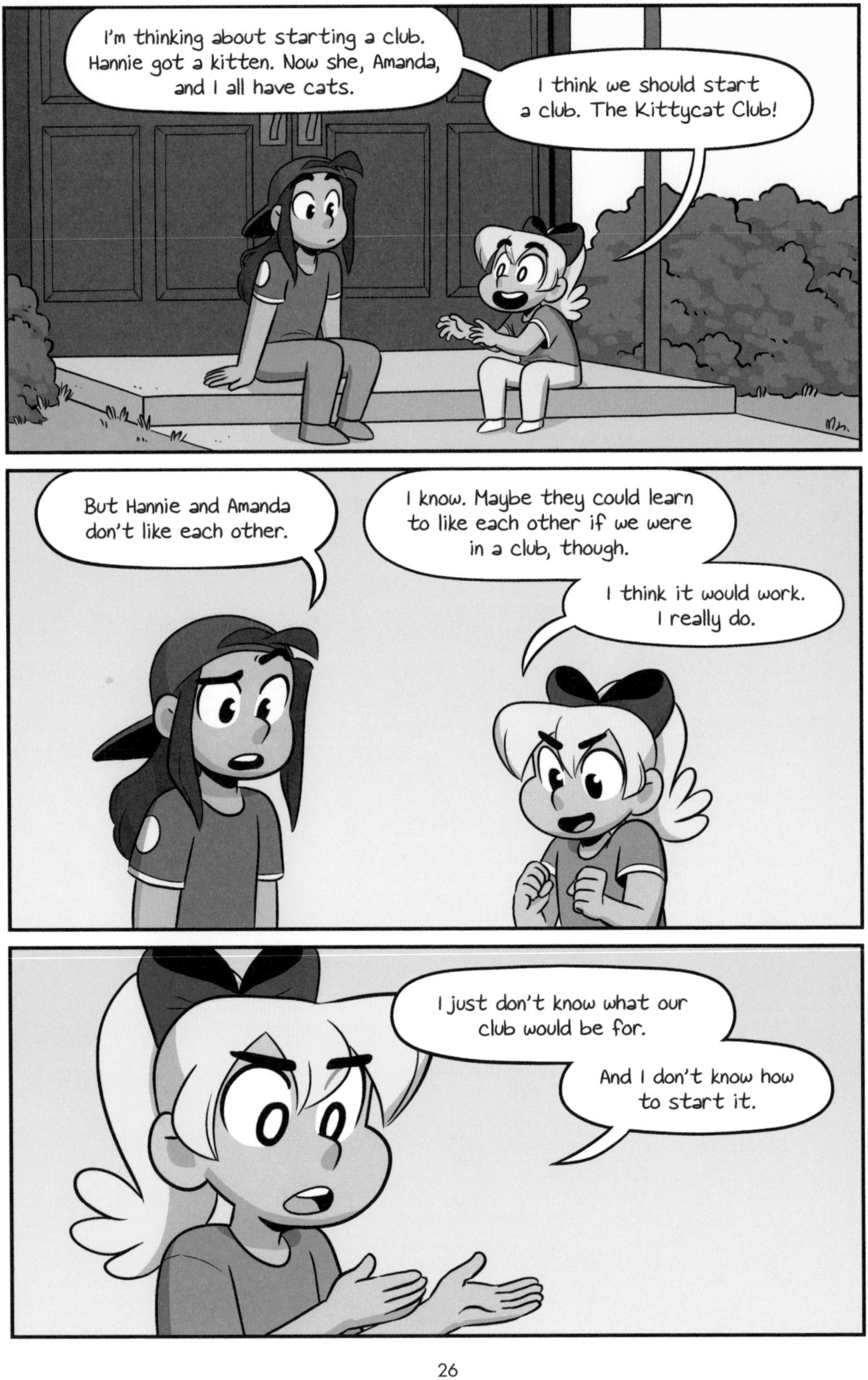
I'm thinking about starting a club. Hannie got a kitten. Now she, Amanda, and I all have cats.
I think we should start a club. The Kittycat Club!
But Hannie and Amanda don't like each other.
I know. Maybe they could learn to like each other if we were in a club, though.
I think it would work. I really do.
I just don't know what our club would be for.
And I don't know how to start it.

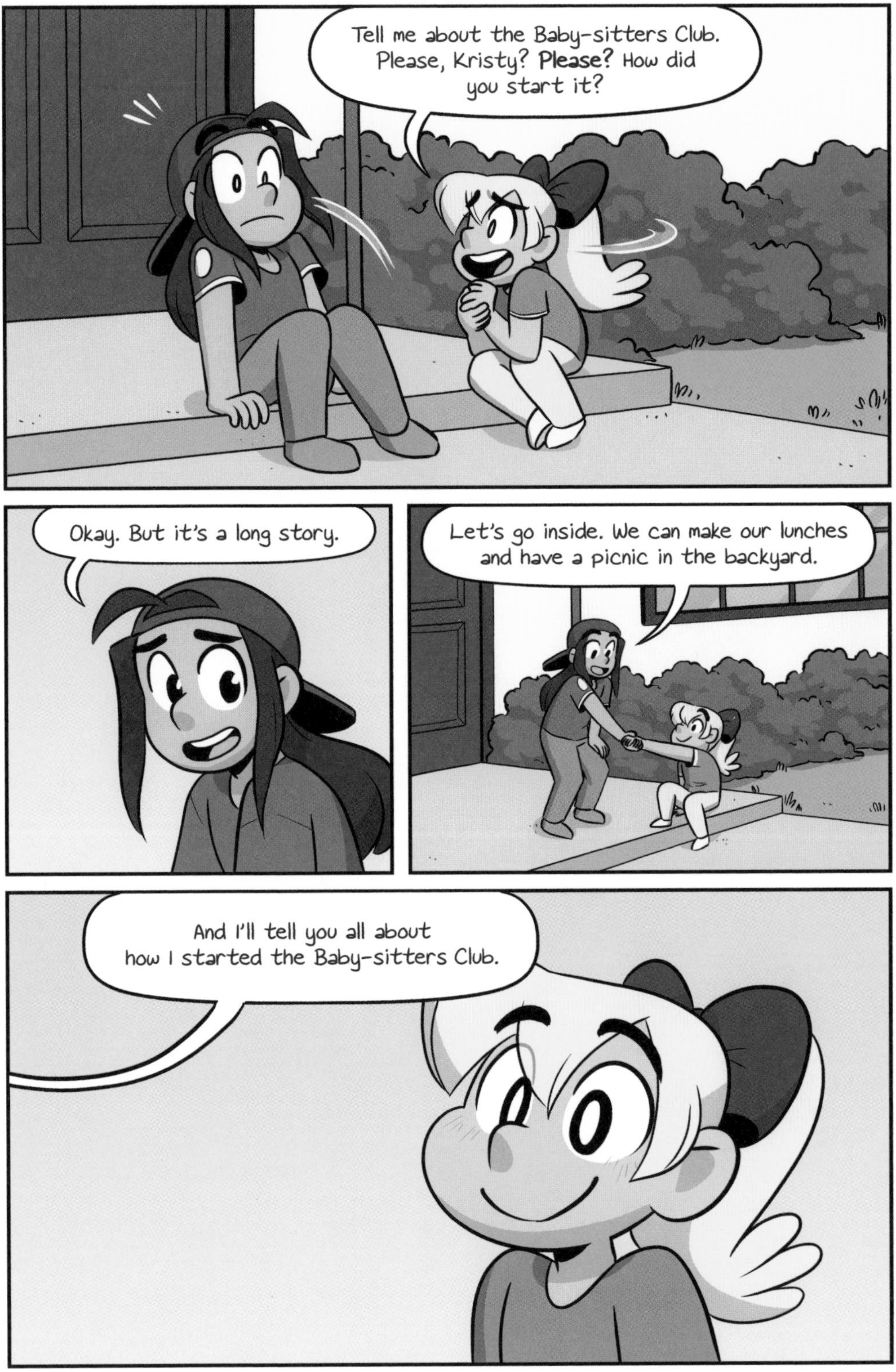

Tell me about the Baby-sitters Club. Please, Kristy? Please? How did you start it?
Okay. But it's a long story.
Let's go inside. We can make our lunches and have a picnic in the backyard.
And I'll tell you all about how I started the Baby-sitters Club.

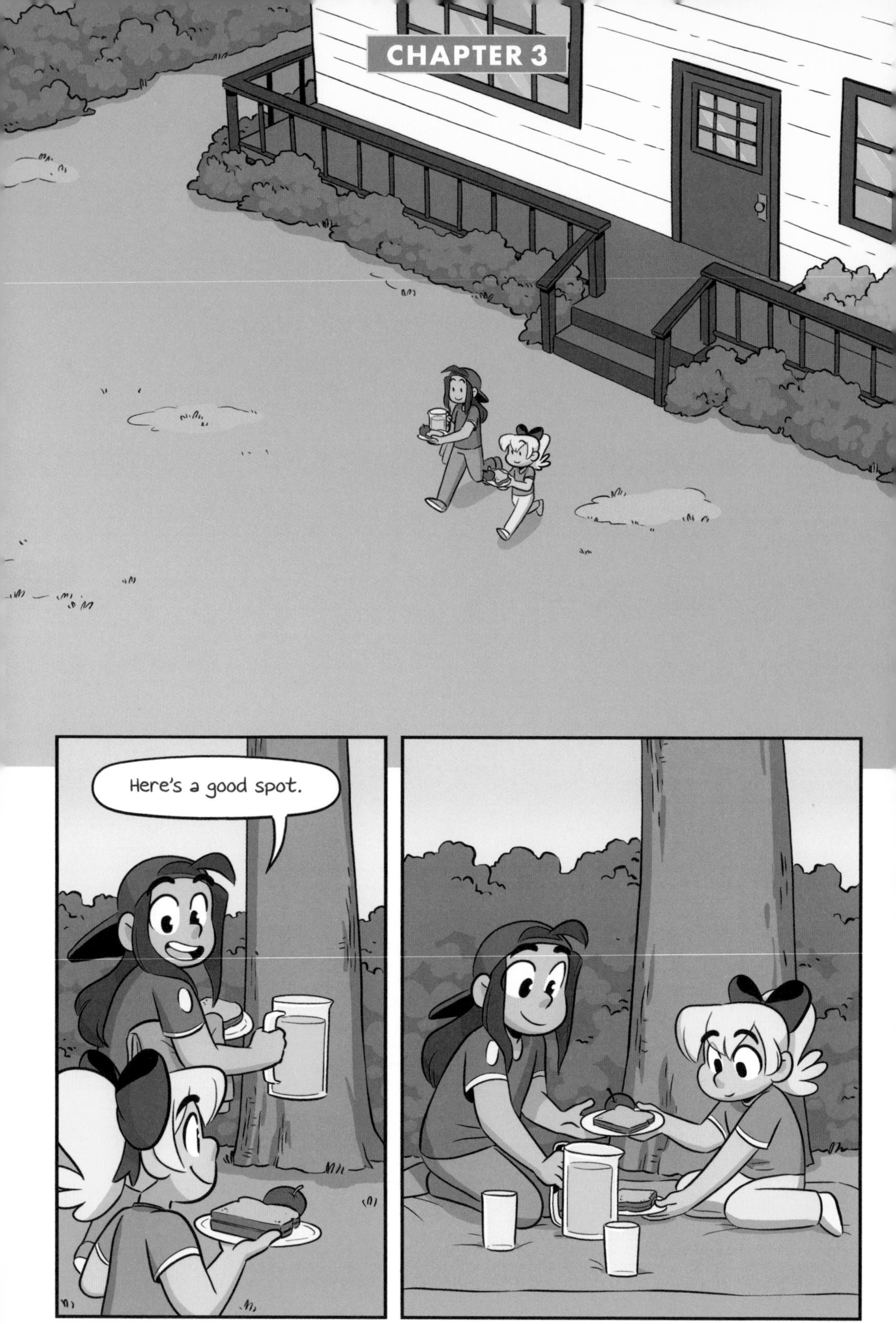
CHAPTER 3
Here's a good spot.

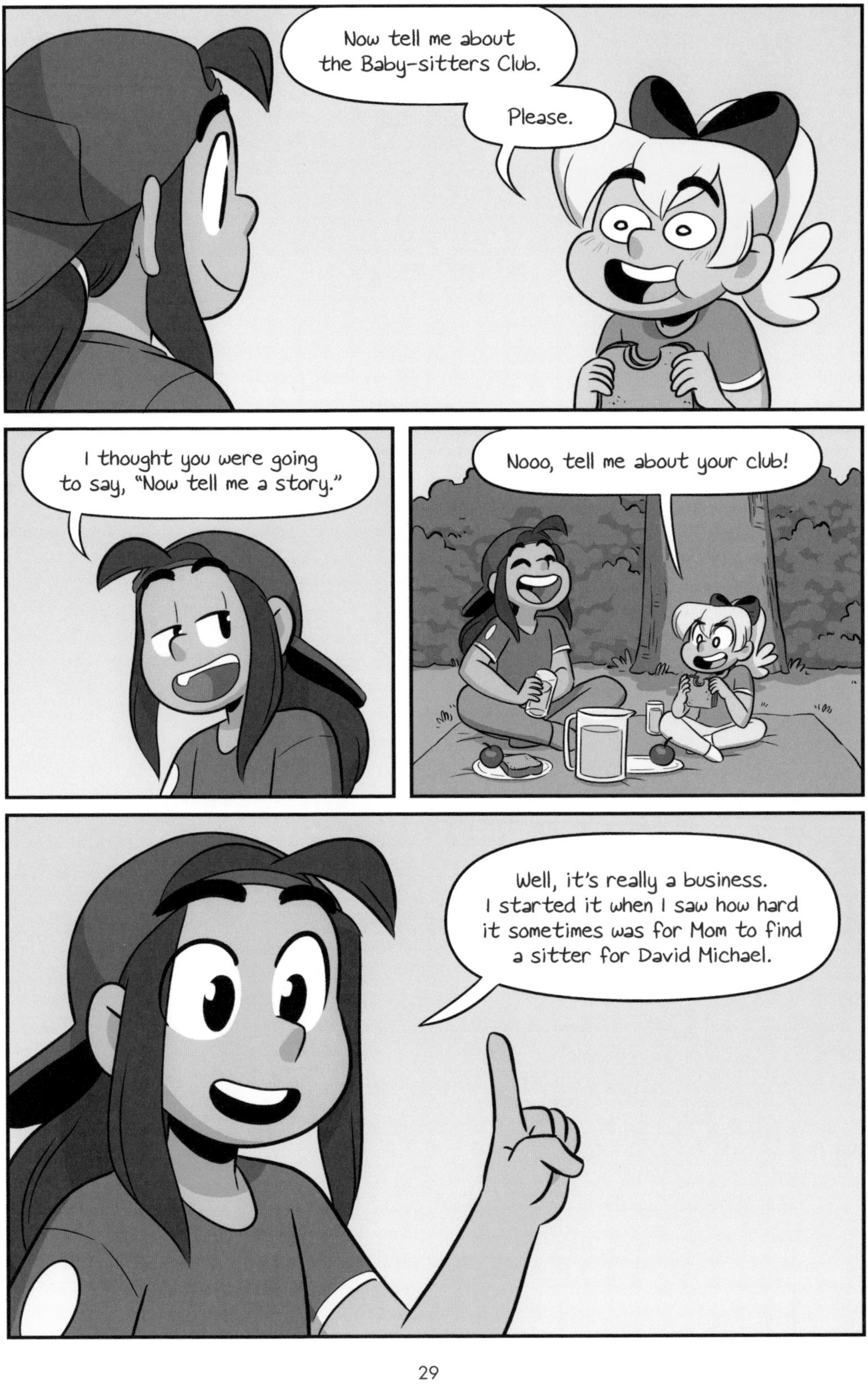
Now tell me about the Baby-sitters Club.
Please.
I thought you were going to say, "Now tell me a story."
Nooo, tell me about your club!
Well, it's really a business. I started it when I saw how hard it sometimes was for Mom to find a sitter for David Michael.

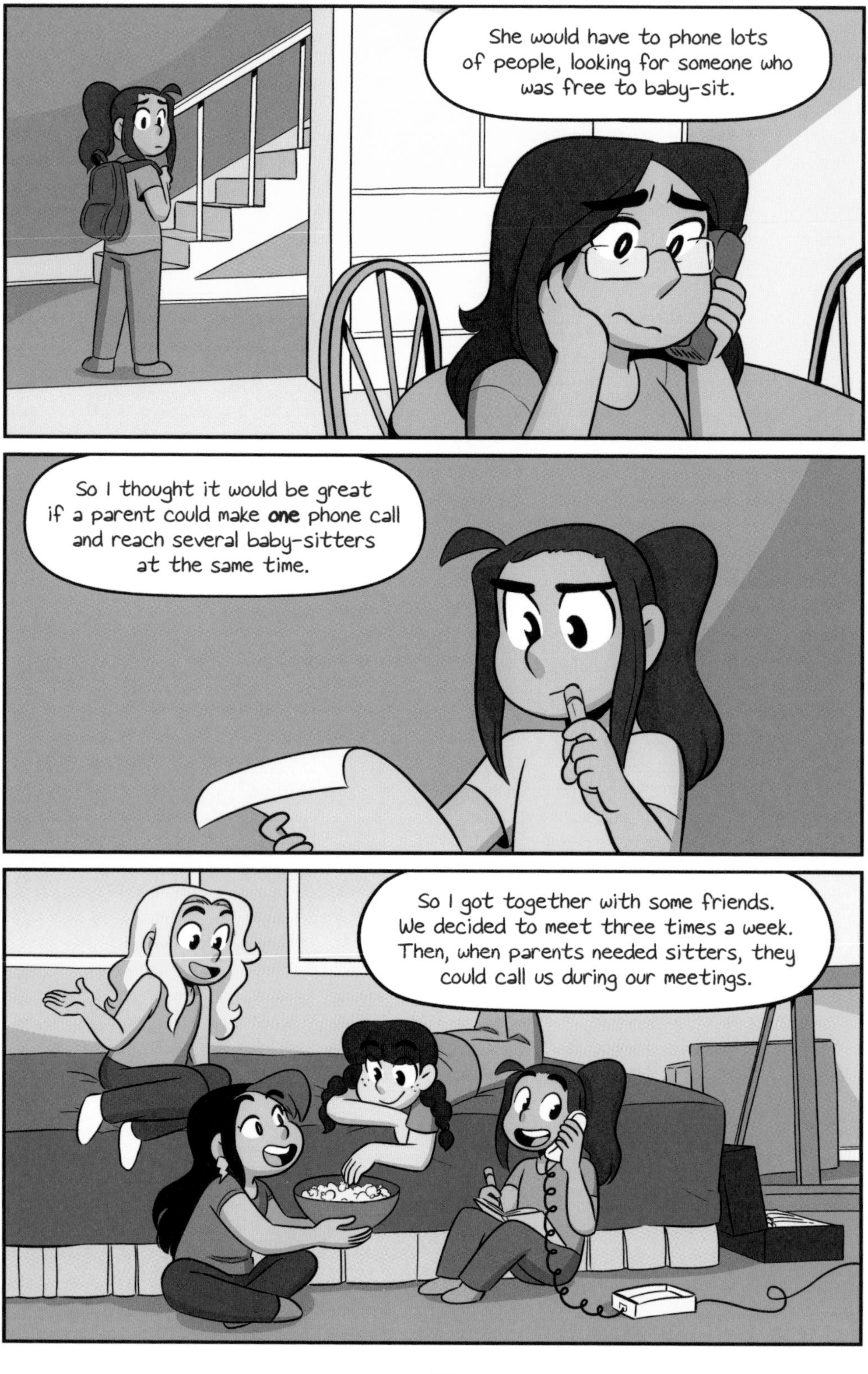
She would have to phone lots of people, looking for someone who was free to baby-sit.
So I thought it would be great if a parent could make **one** phone call and reach several baby-sitters at the same time.
So I got together with some friends. We decided to meet three times a week. Then, when parents needed sitters, they could call us during our meetings.

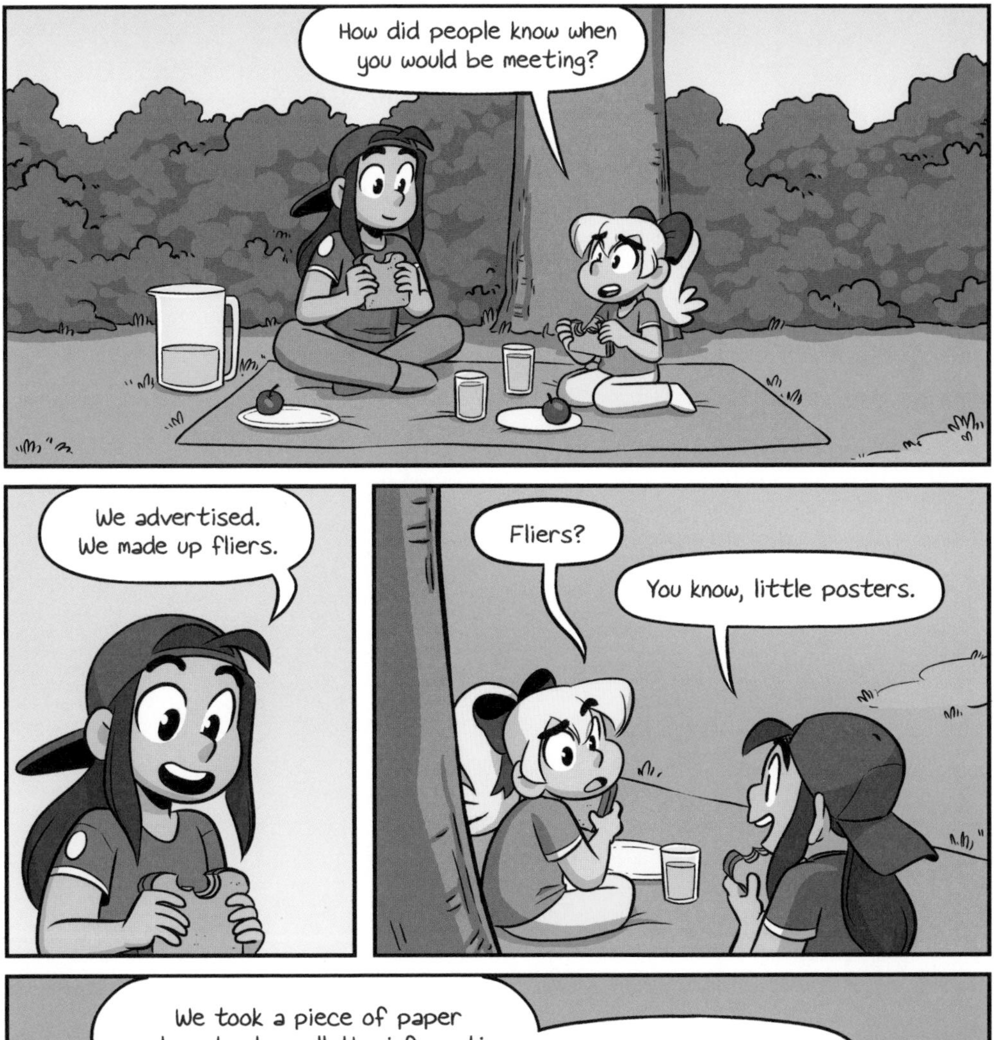
How did people know when you would be meeting?
We advertised. We made up fliers.
Fliers?
You know, little posters.
We took a piece of paper and wrote down all the information about the club.
Things like what we do, when we meet, and how to reach us.
Need a baby-sitter? Save time
CALL
B
S
C
The Baby-sitters Club
CALL NOW!
Available:
Weekends
After School
Evenings
Need a baby-sitter? Save time
CALL
B
S
C
The Baby-sitters Club
CALL NOW!
Weekends
After School

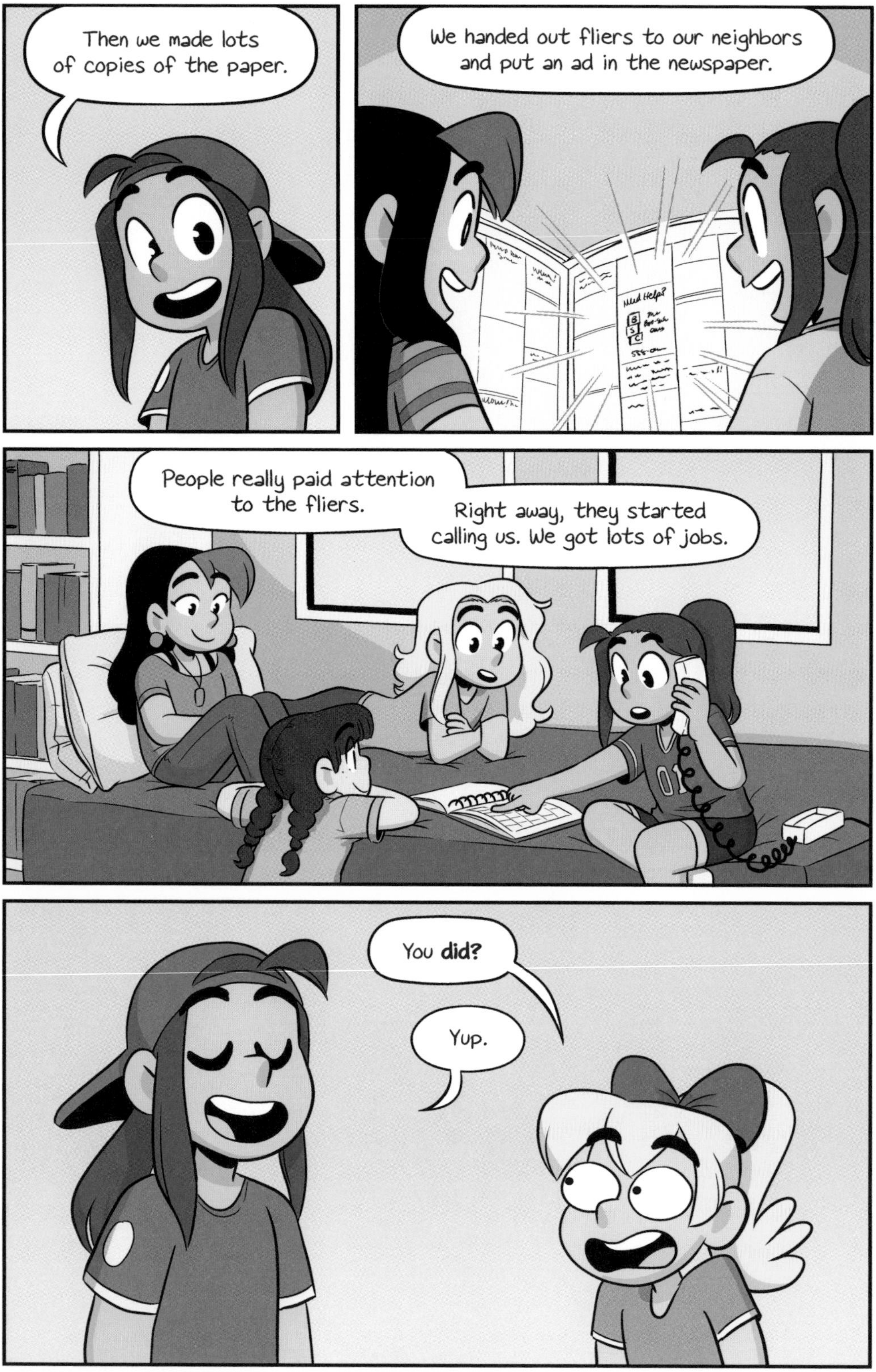
Then we made lots of copies of the paper.
We handed out fliers to our neighbors and put an ad in the newspaper.
People really paid attention to the fliers.
Right away, they started calling us. We got lots of jobs.
You **did?**
Yup.

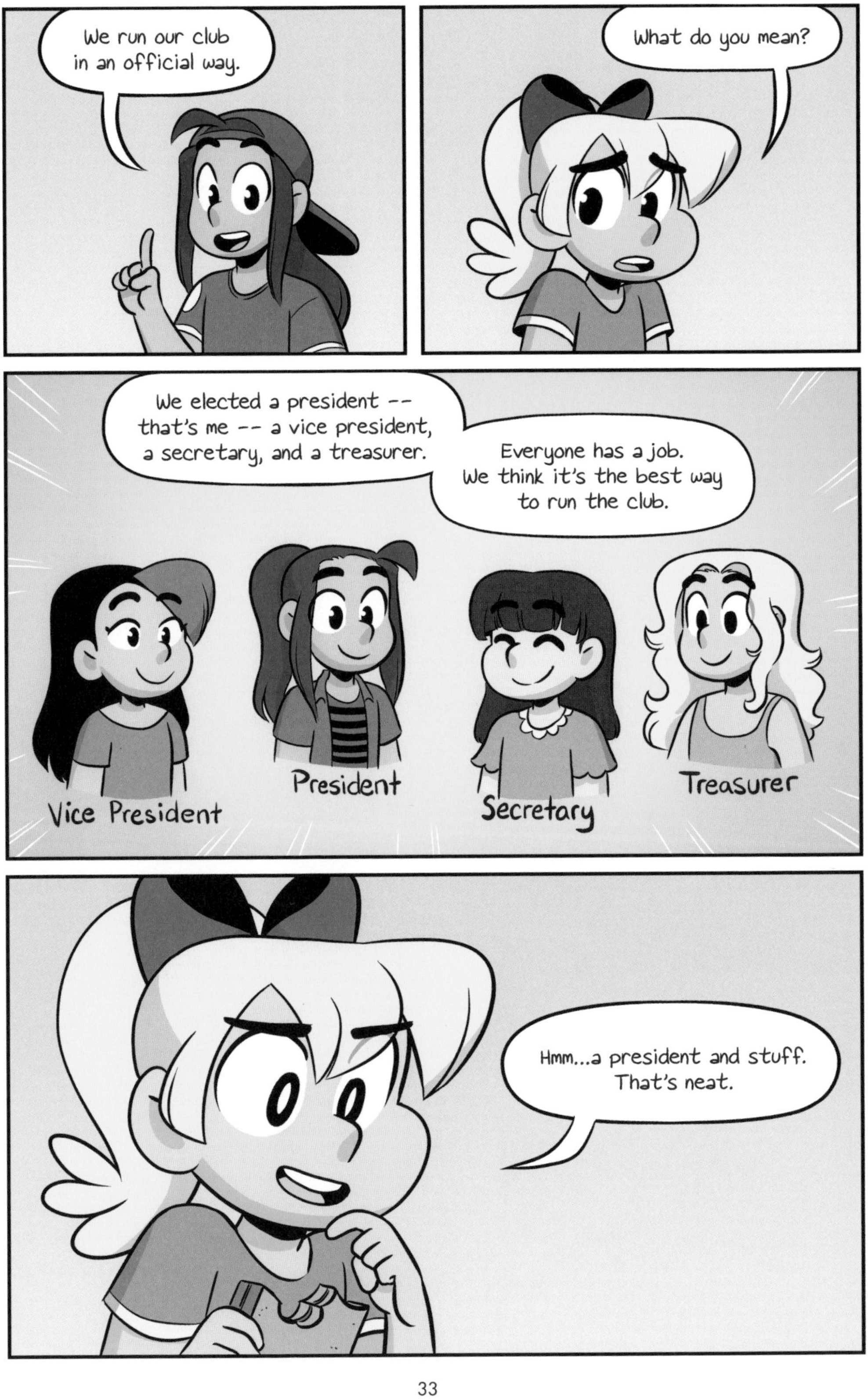
We run our club in an official way.
What do you mean?
We elected a president -- that's me -- a vice president, a secretary, and a treasurer.
Everyone has a job. We think it's the best way to run the club.
Vice President
President
Secretary
Treasurer
Hmm...a president and stuff. That's neat.

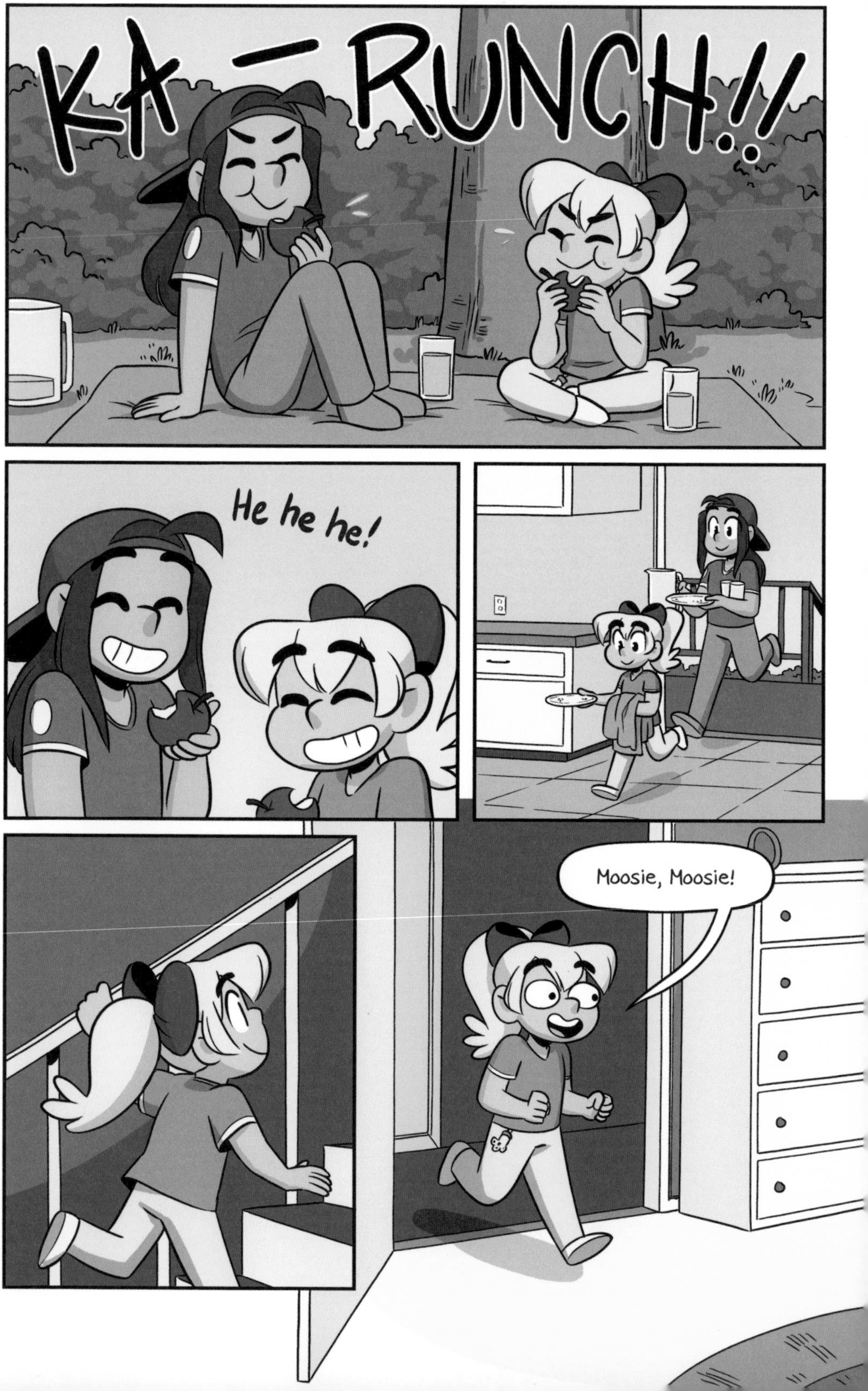
KA-RUNCH!!
He he he!
Moosie, Moosie!

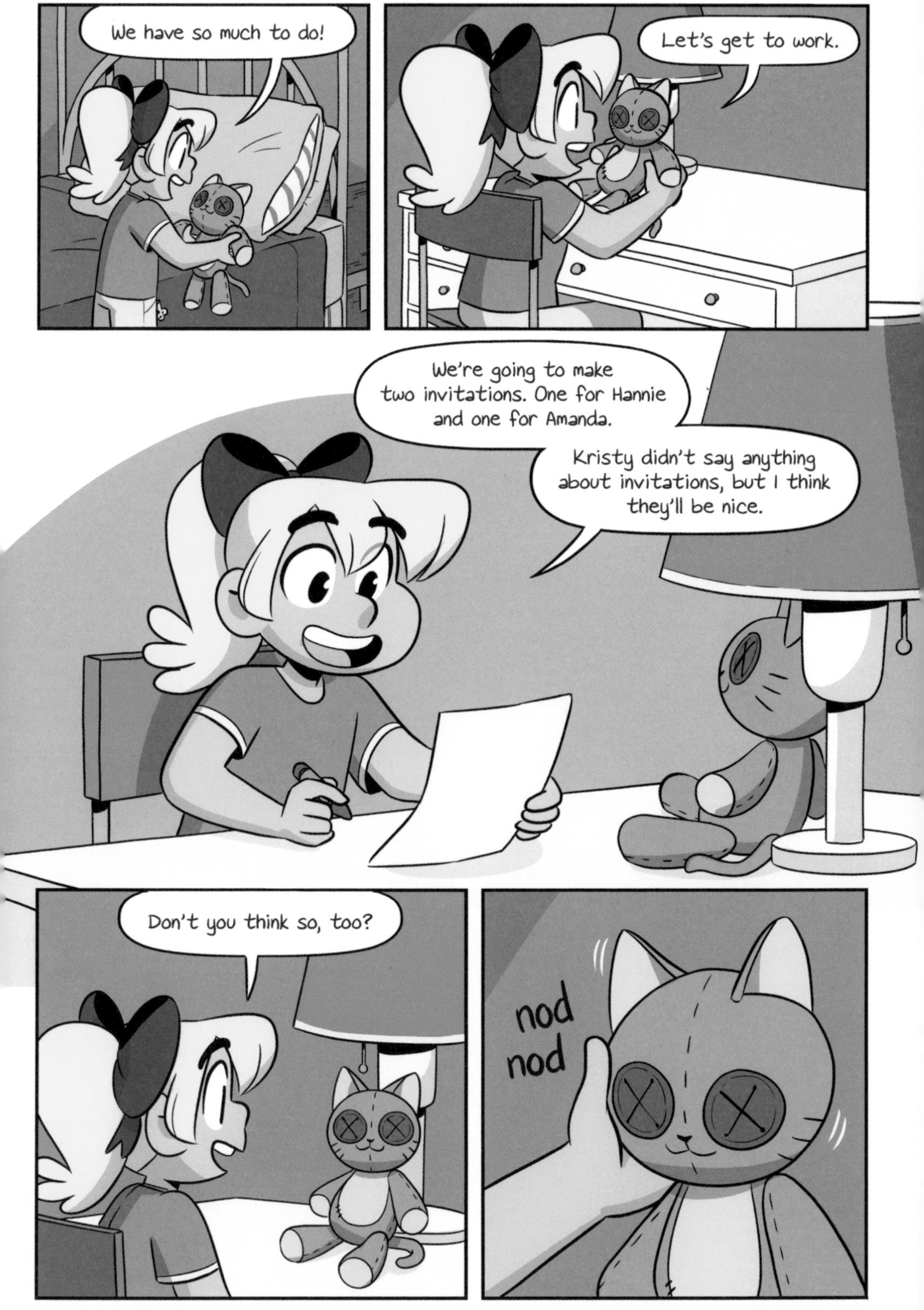
We have so much to do!
Let's get to work.
We're going to make two invitations. One for Hannie and one for Amanda.
Kristy didn't say anything about invitations, but I think they'll be nice.
Don't you think so, too?
nod nod

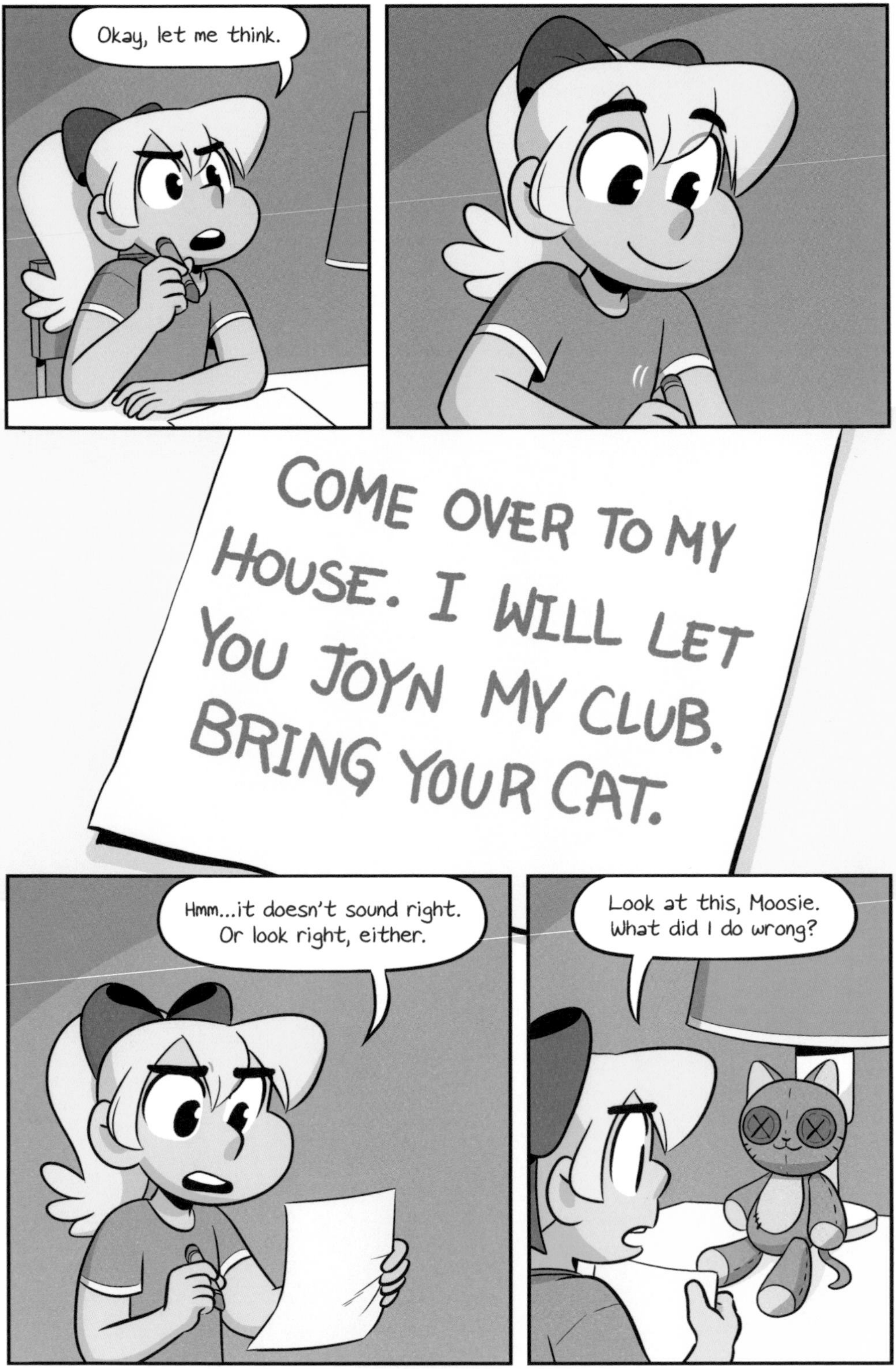
Okay, let me think.
COME OVER TO MY HOUSE. I WILL LET YOU JOYN MY CLUB. BRING YOUR CAT.
Hmm...it doesn't sound right. Or look right, either.
Look at this, Moosie. What did I do wrong?

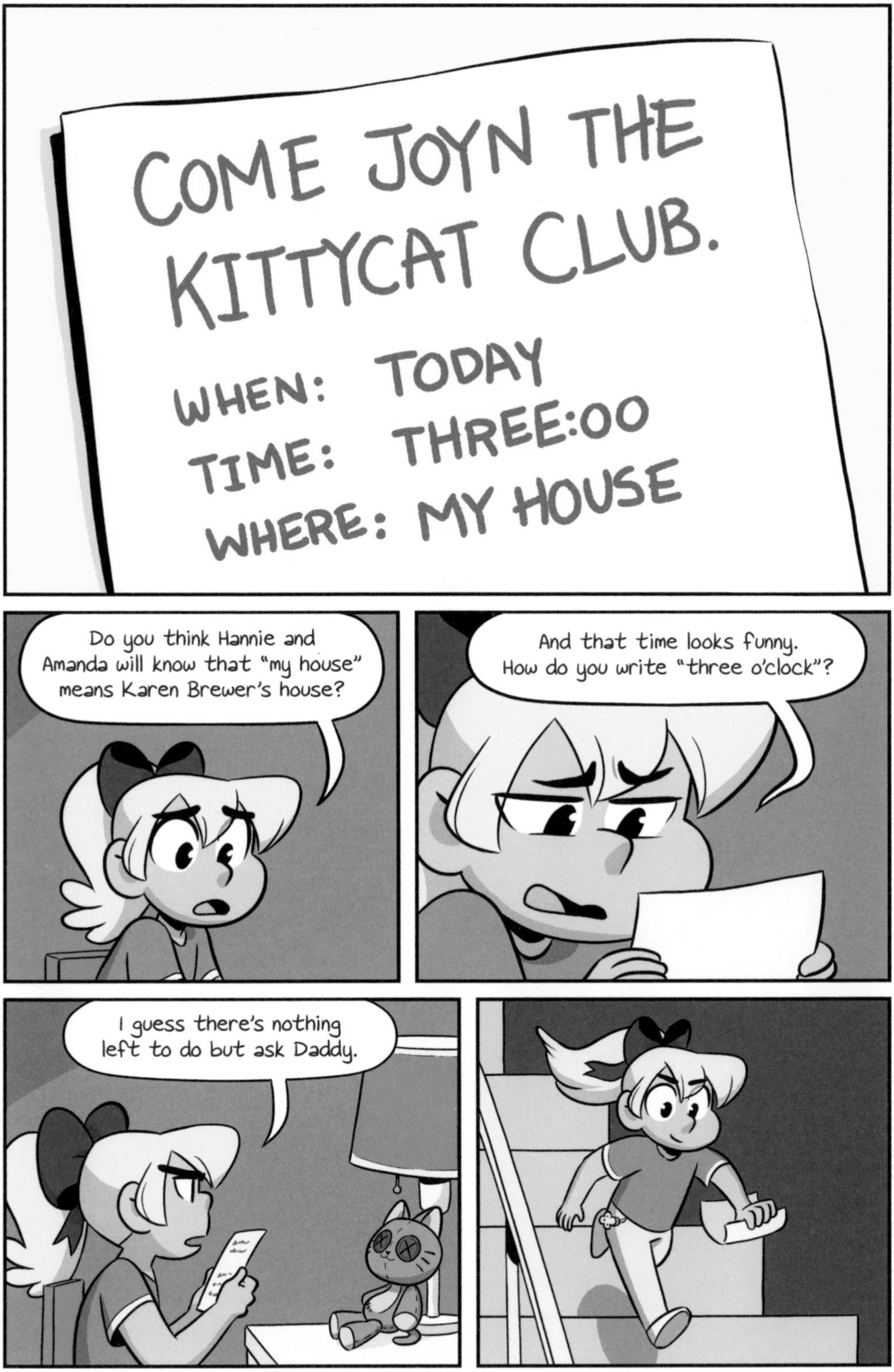
COME JOYN THE KITTYCAT CLUB.
WHEN: TODAY
TIME: THREE:00
WHERE: MY HOUSE
Do you think Hannie and Amanda will know that "my house" means Karen Brewer's house?
And that time looks funny. How do you write "three o'clock"?
I guess there's nothing left to do but ask Daddy.

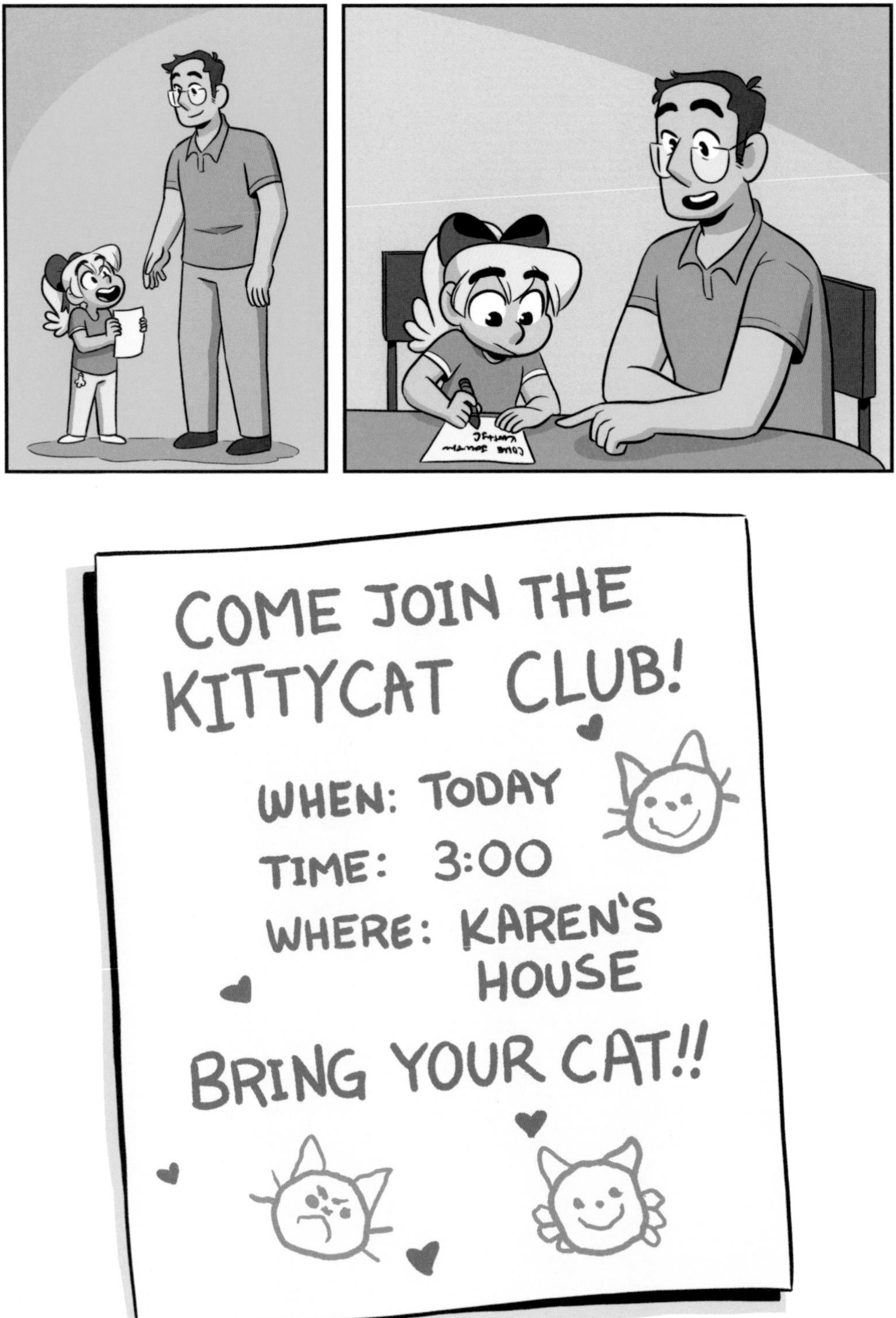
COME JOIN THE KITTYCAT CLUB!
WHEN: TODAY
TIME: 3:00
WHERE: KAREN'S HOUSE
BRING YOUR CAT!!

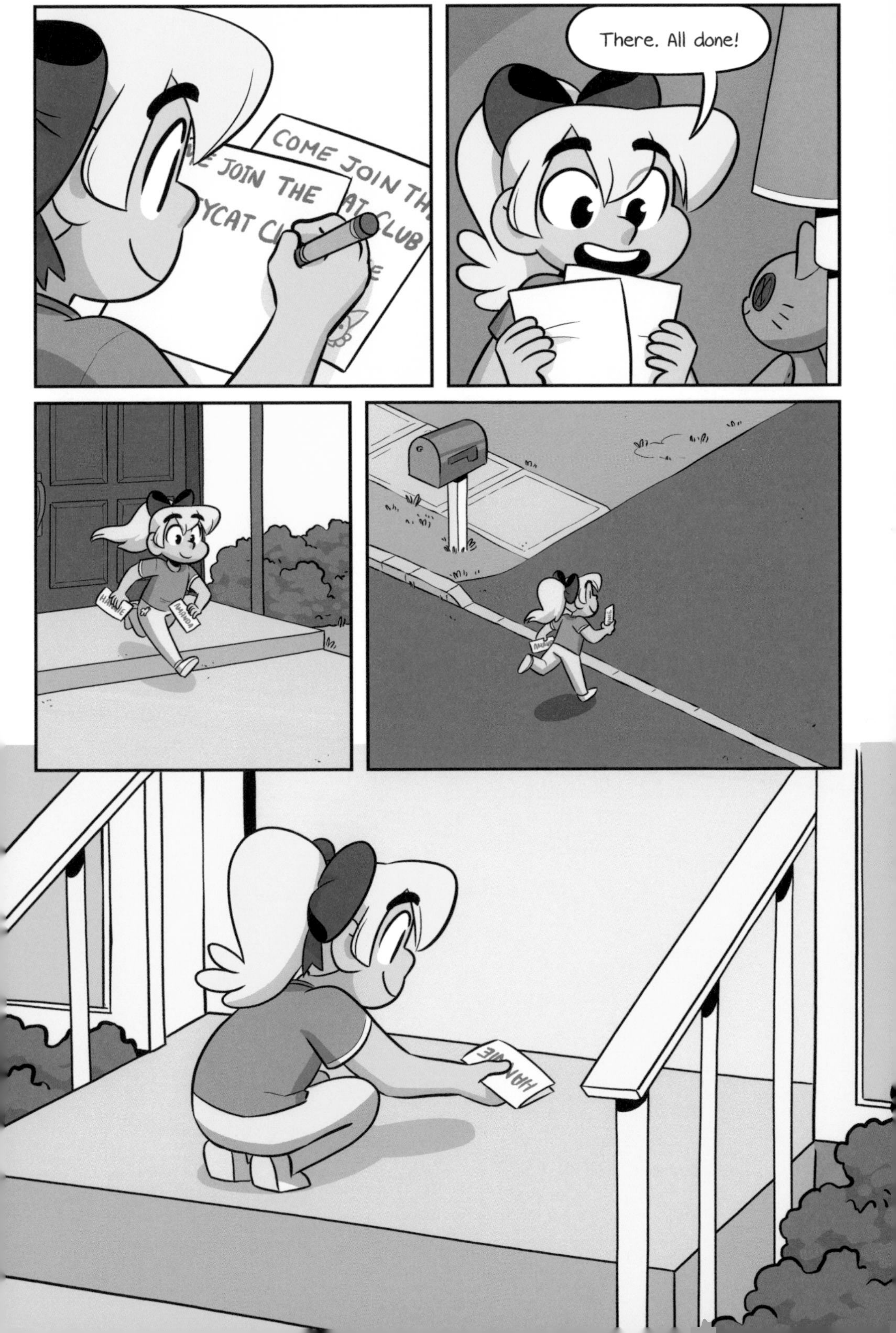
There. All done!

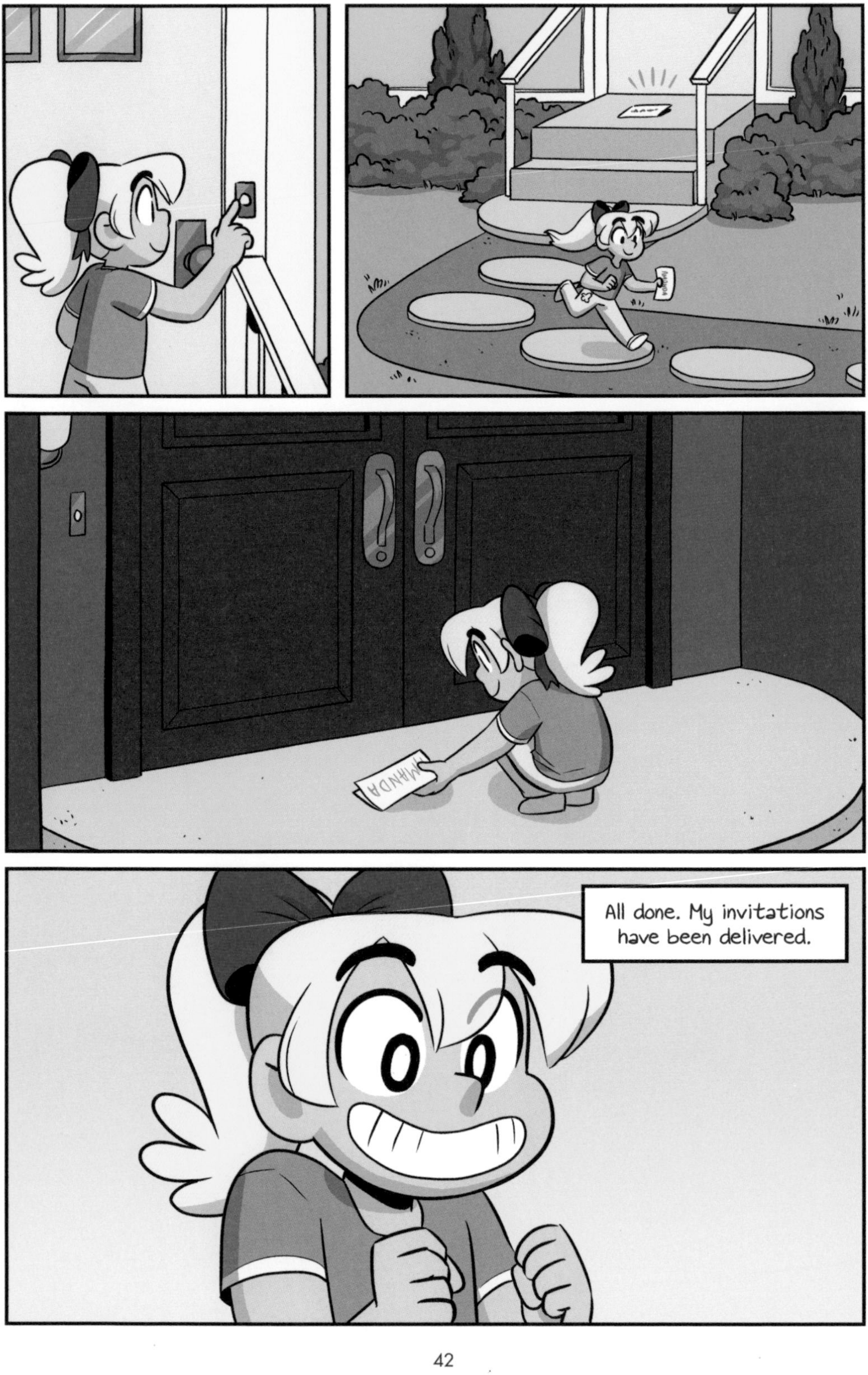
MANDA
All done. My invitations have been delivered.

CHAPTER 4

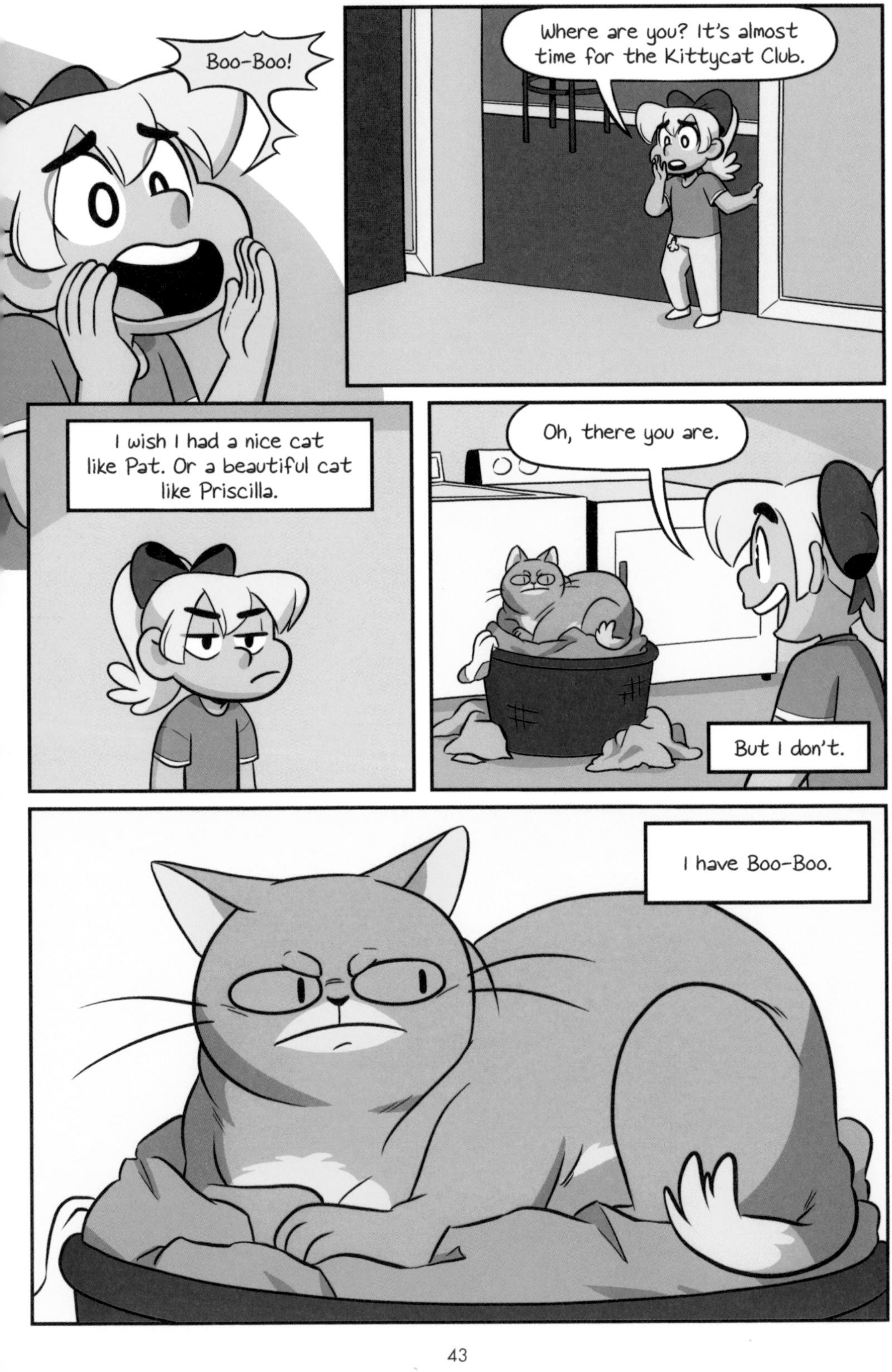

Boo-Boo!
Where are you? It's almost time for the Kittycat Club.
I wish I had a nice cat like Pat. Or a beautiful cat like Priscilla.
Oh, there you are.
But I don't.
I have Boo-Boo.

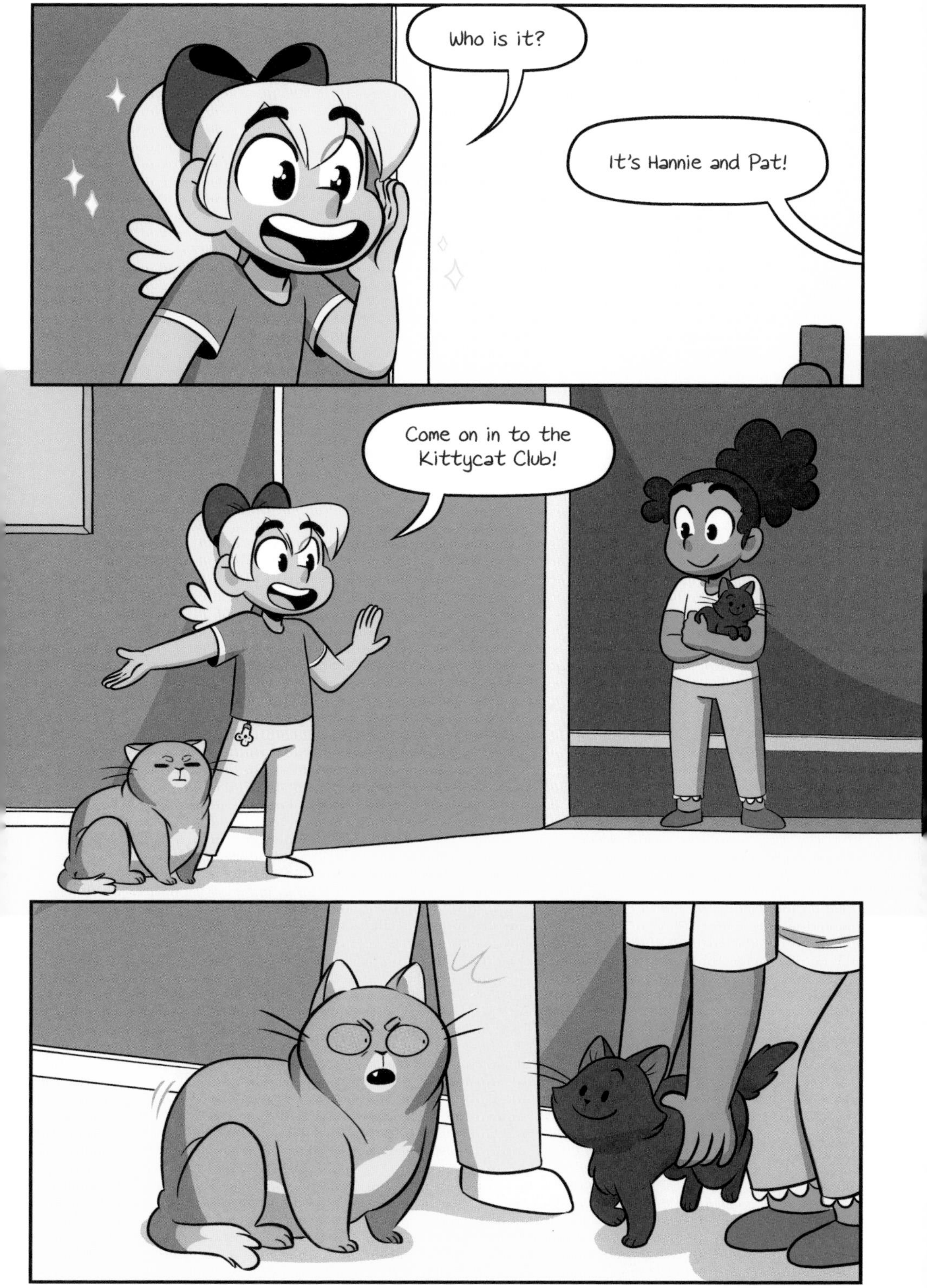
Who is it?
It's Hannie and Pat!
Come on in to the Kittycat Club!

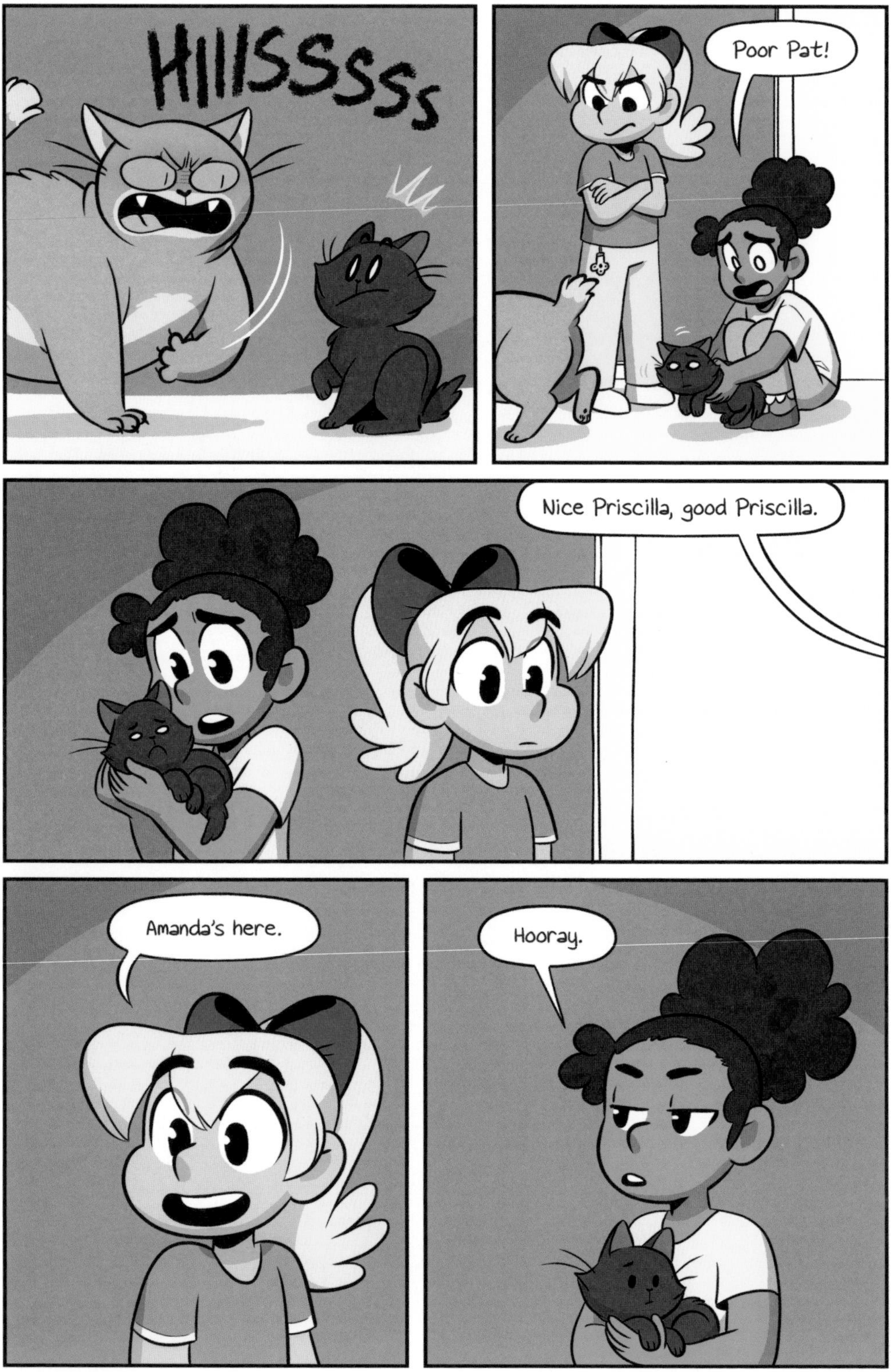
HIIISSSSSS
Poor Pat!
Nice Priscilla, good Priscilla.
Amanda's here.
Hooray.

47

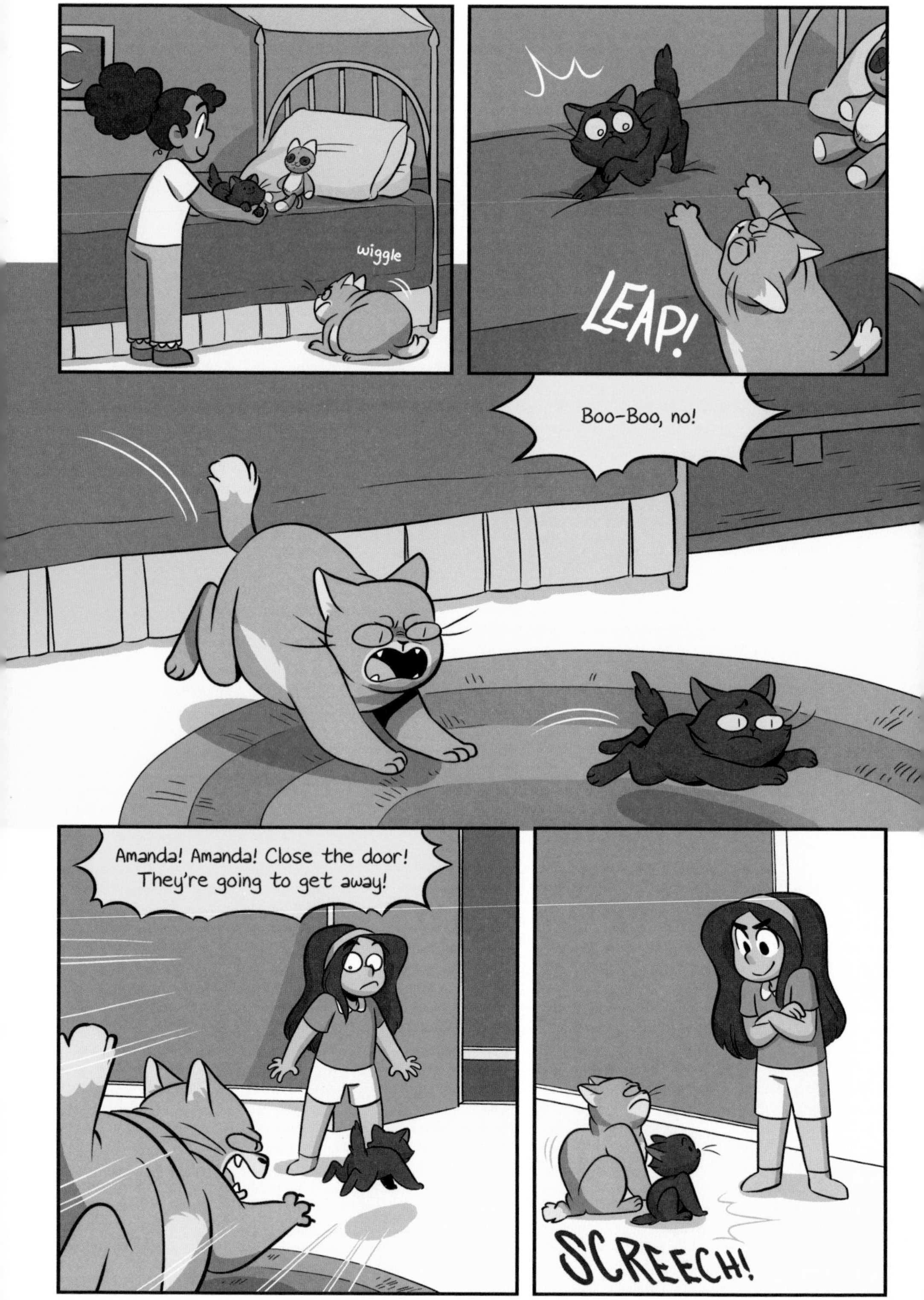
wiggle
LEAP!
Boo-Boo, no!
Amanda! Amanda! Close the door! They're going to get away!
SCREECH!

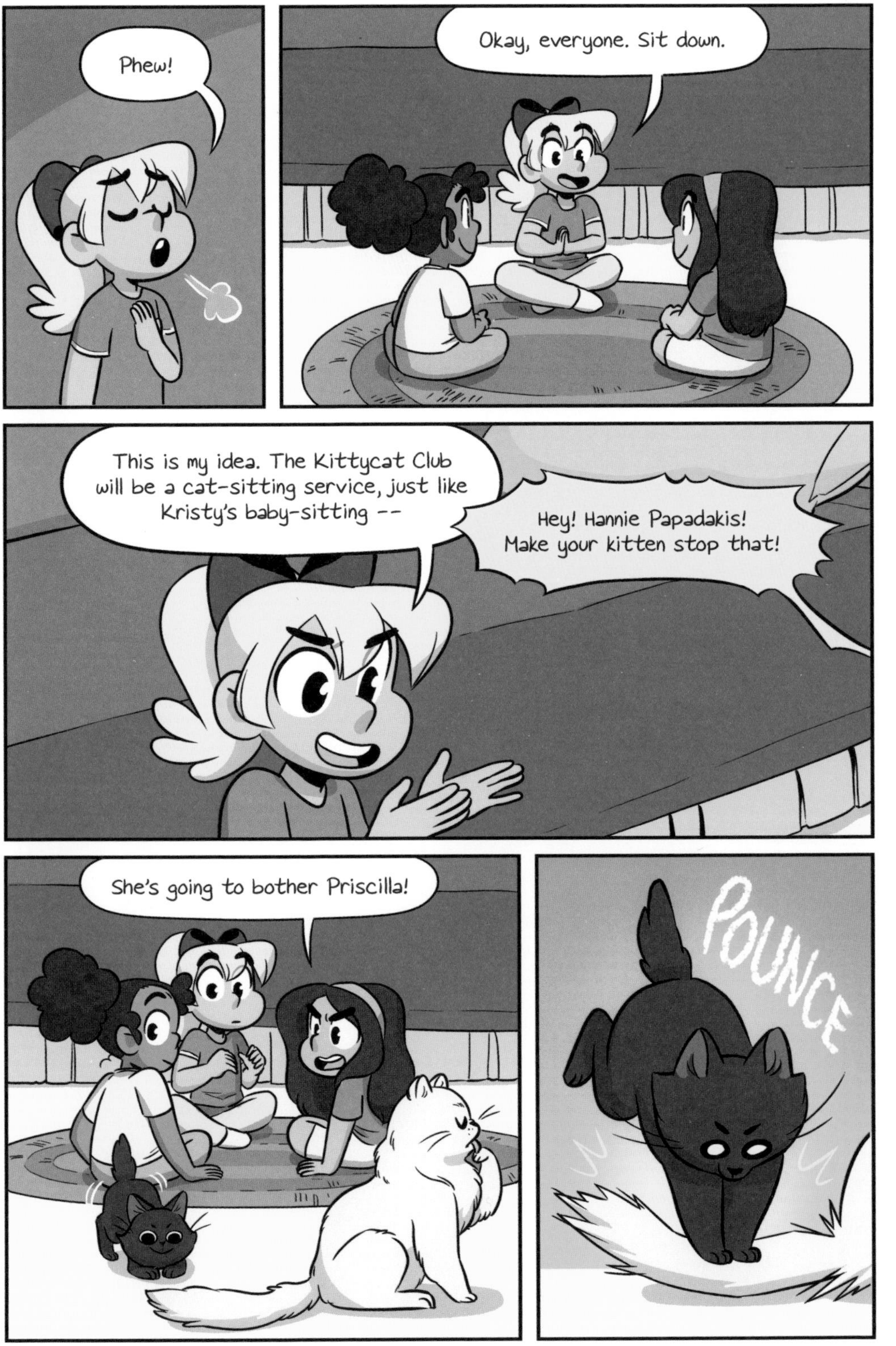
Phew!
Okay, everyone. Sit down.
This is my idea. The Kittycat Club will be a cat-sitting service, just like Kristy's baby-sitting --
Hey! Hannie Papadakis! Make your kitten stop that!
She's going to bother Priscilla!
POUNCE

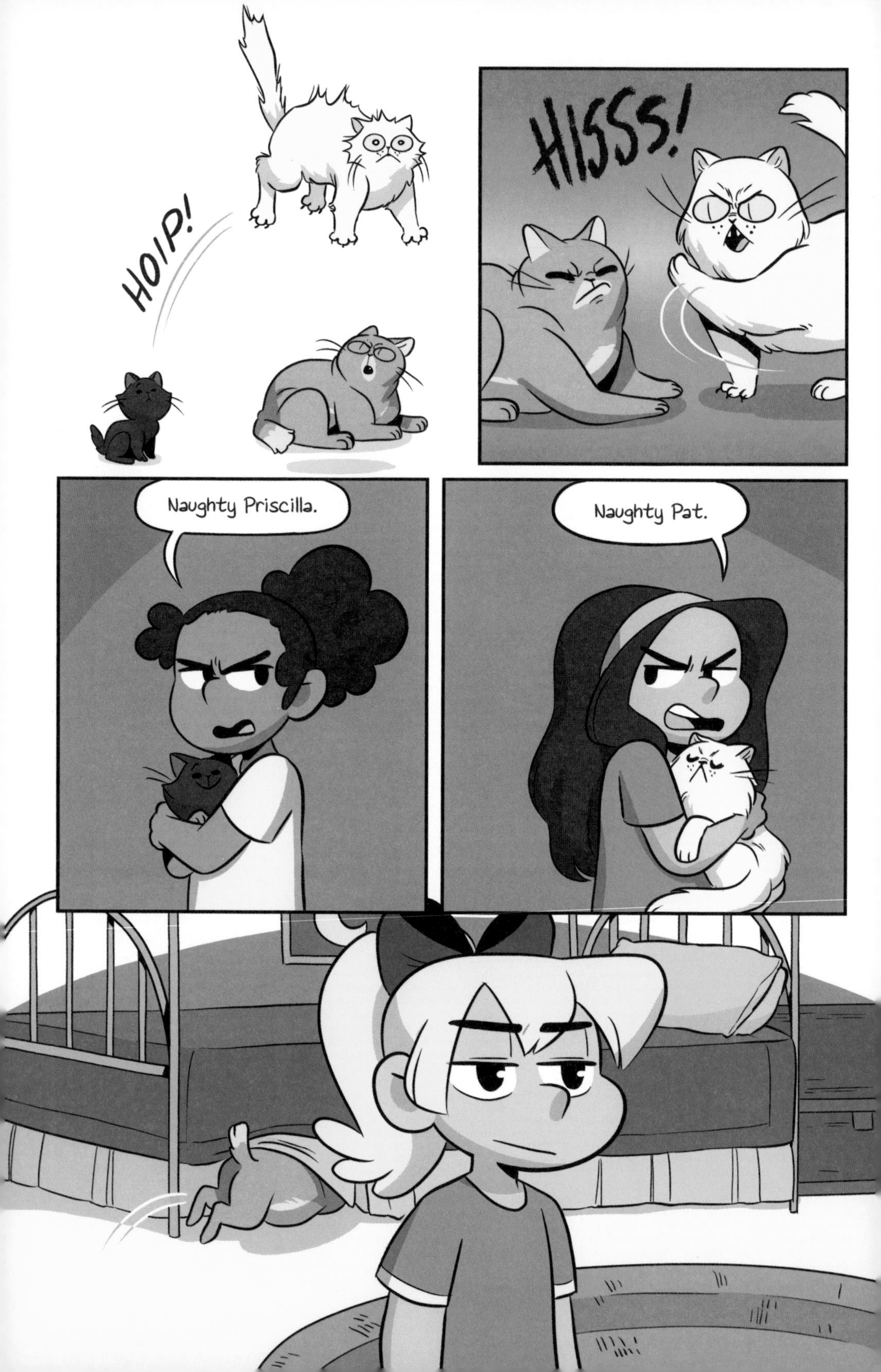
HOIP!
HISSS!
Naughty Priscilla.
Naughty Pat.

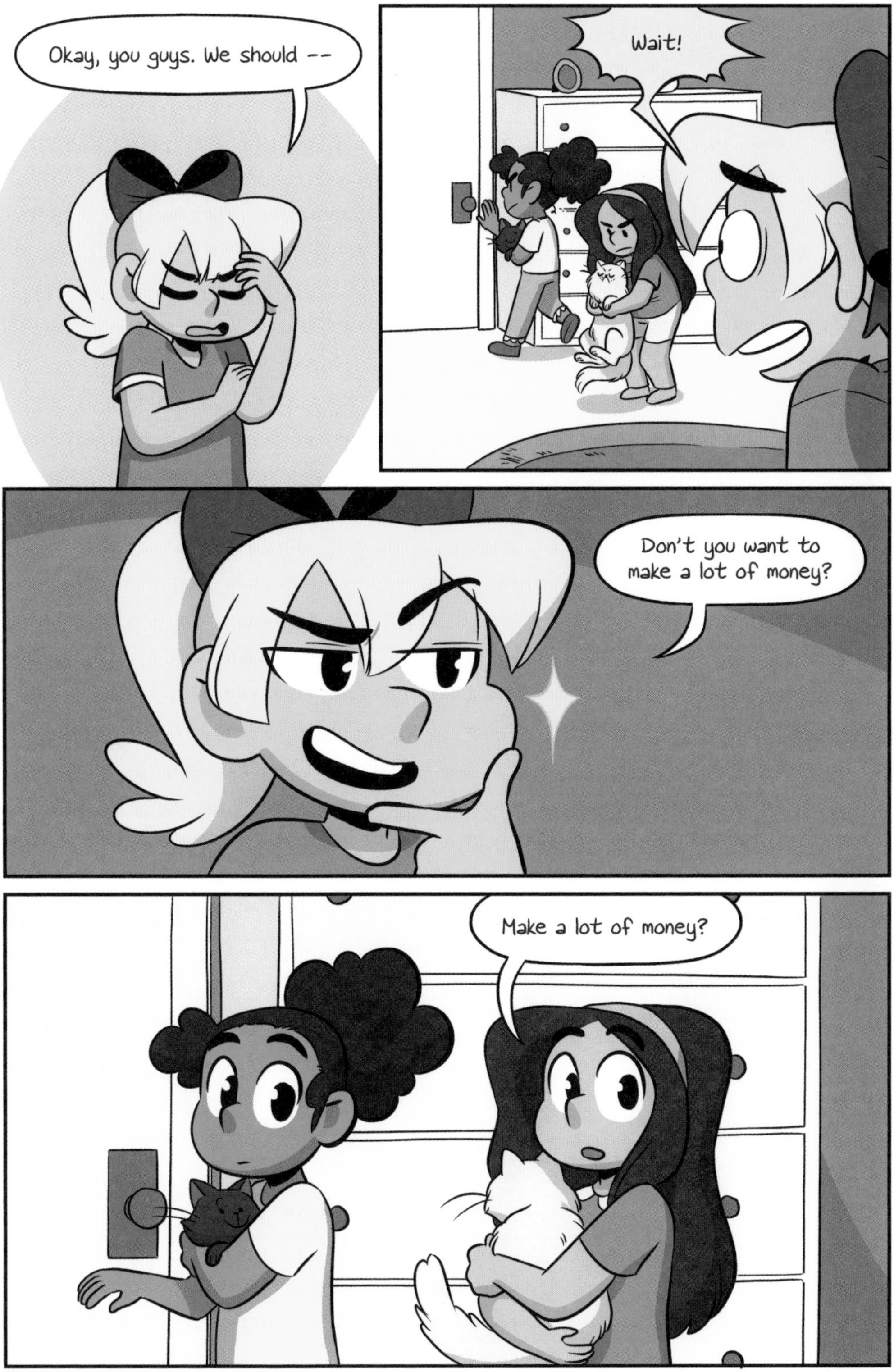
Okay, you guys. We should --
Wait!
Don't you want to make a lot of money?
Make a lot of money?

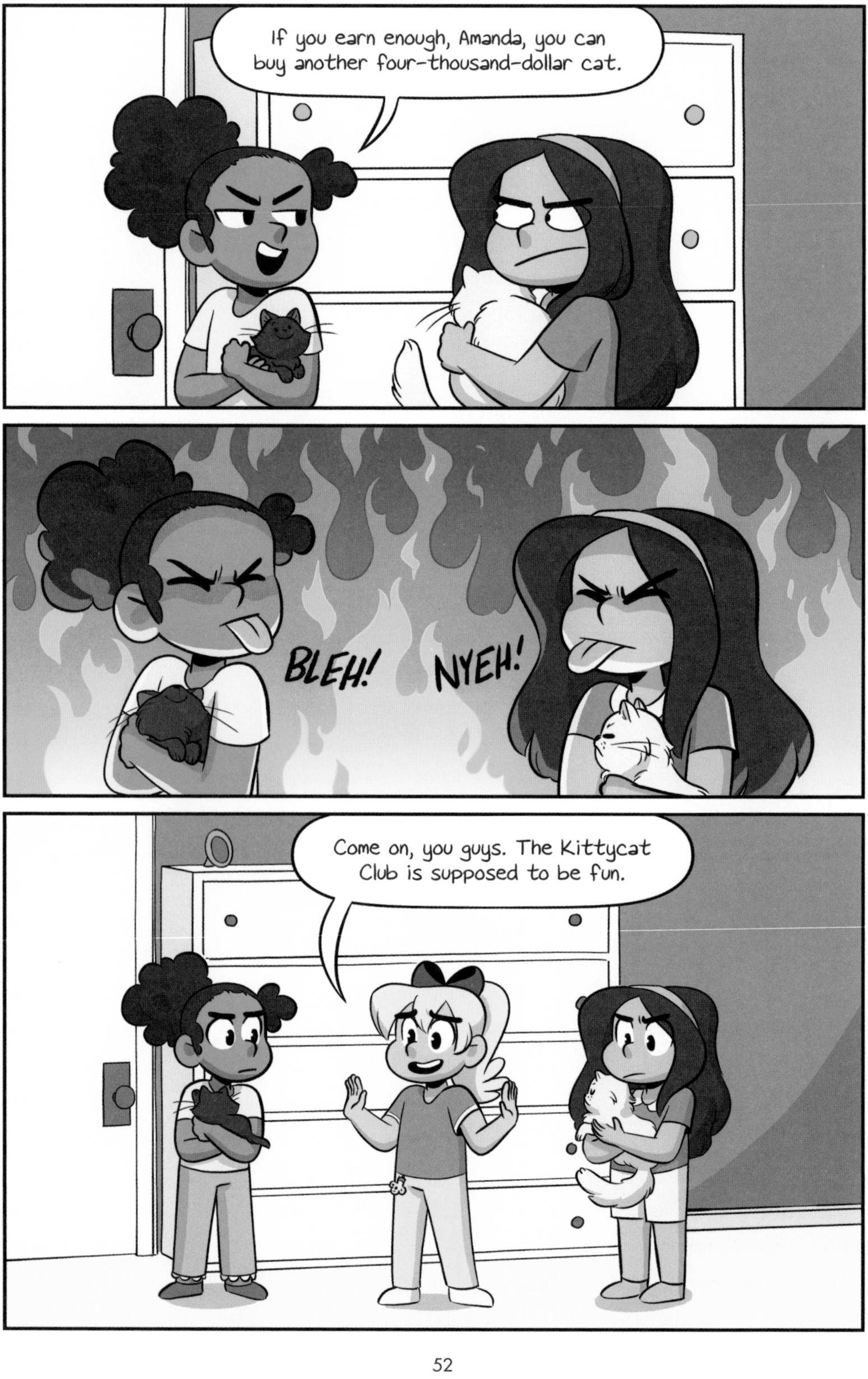
If you earn enough, Amanda, you can buy another four-thousand-dollar cat.
BLEH!
NYEH!
Come on, you guys. The Kittycat Club is supposed to be fun.

56

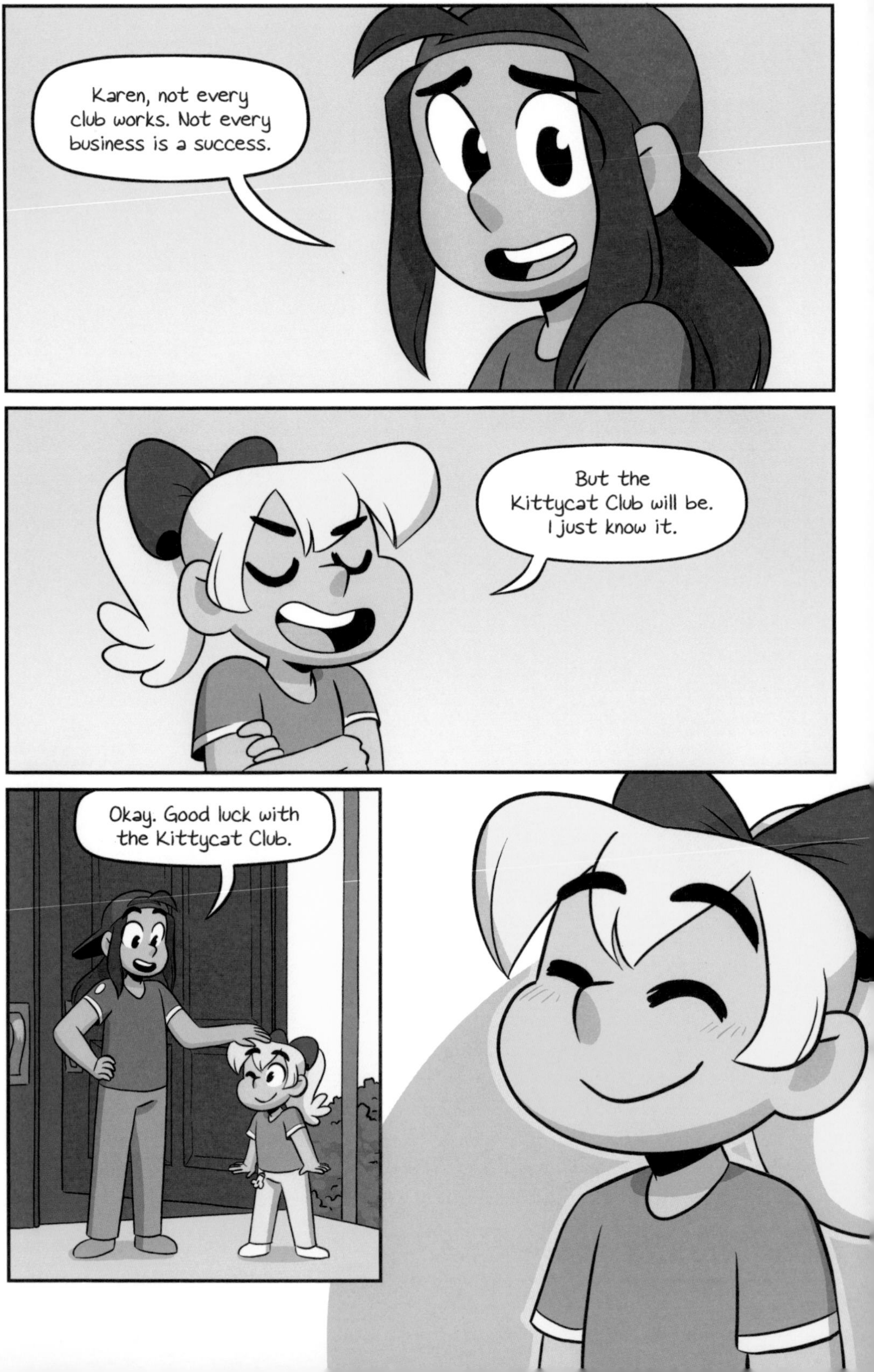
Karen, not every club works. Not every business is a success.
But the Kittycat Club will be. I just know it.
Okay. Good luck with the Kittycat Club.

CHAPTER 5

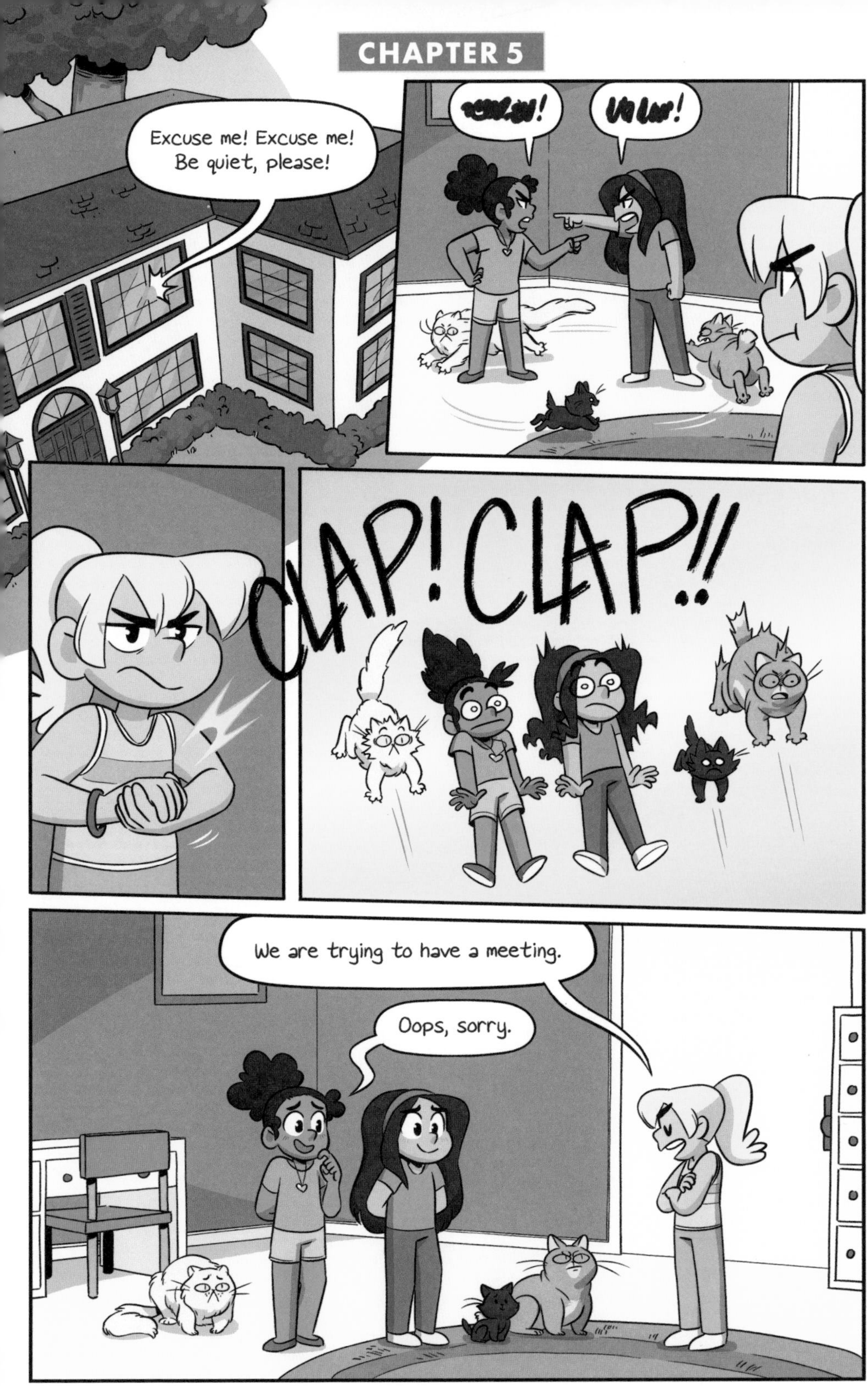

Excuse me! Excuse me! Be quiet, please!
CLAP! CLAP!!
We are trying to have a meeting.
Oops, sorry.

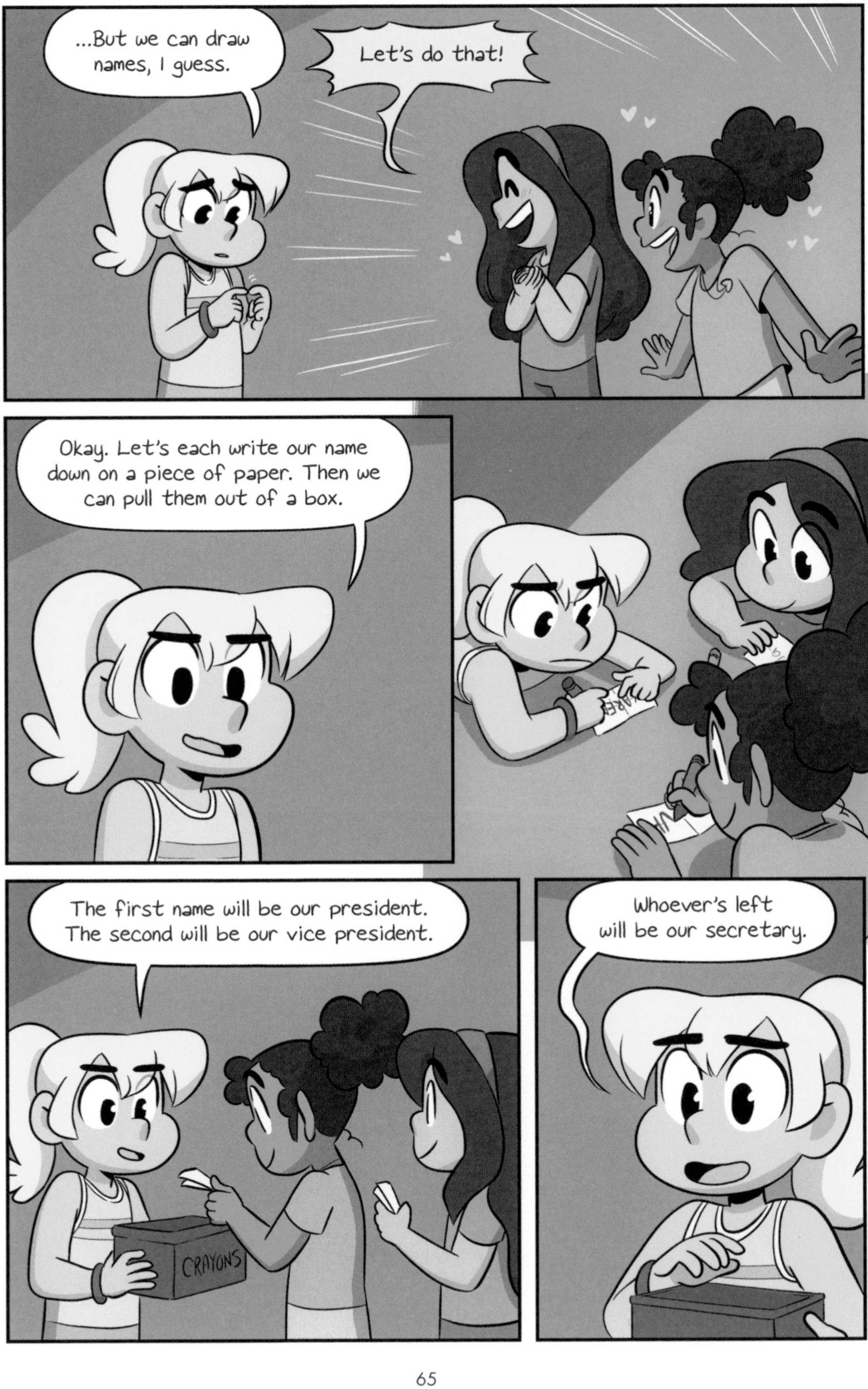
...But we can draw names, I guess.
Let's do that!
Okay. Let's each write our name down on a piece of paper. Then we can pull them out of a box.
The first name will be our president. The second will be our vice president.
CRAYONS
Whoever's left will be our secretary.

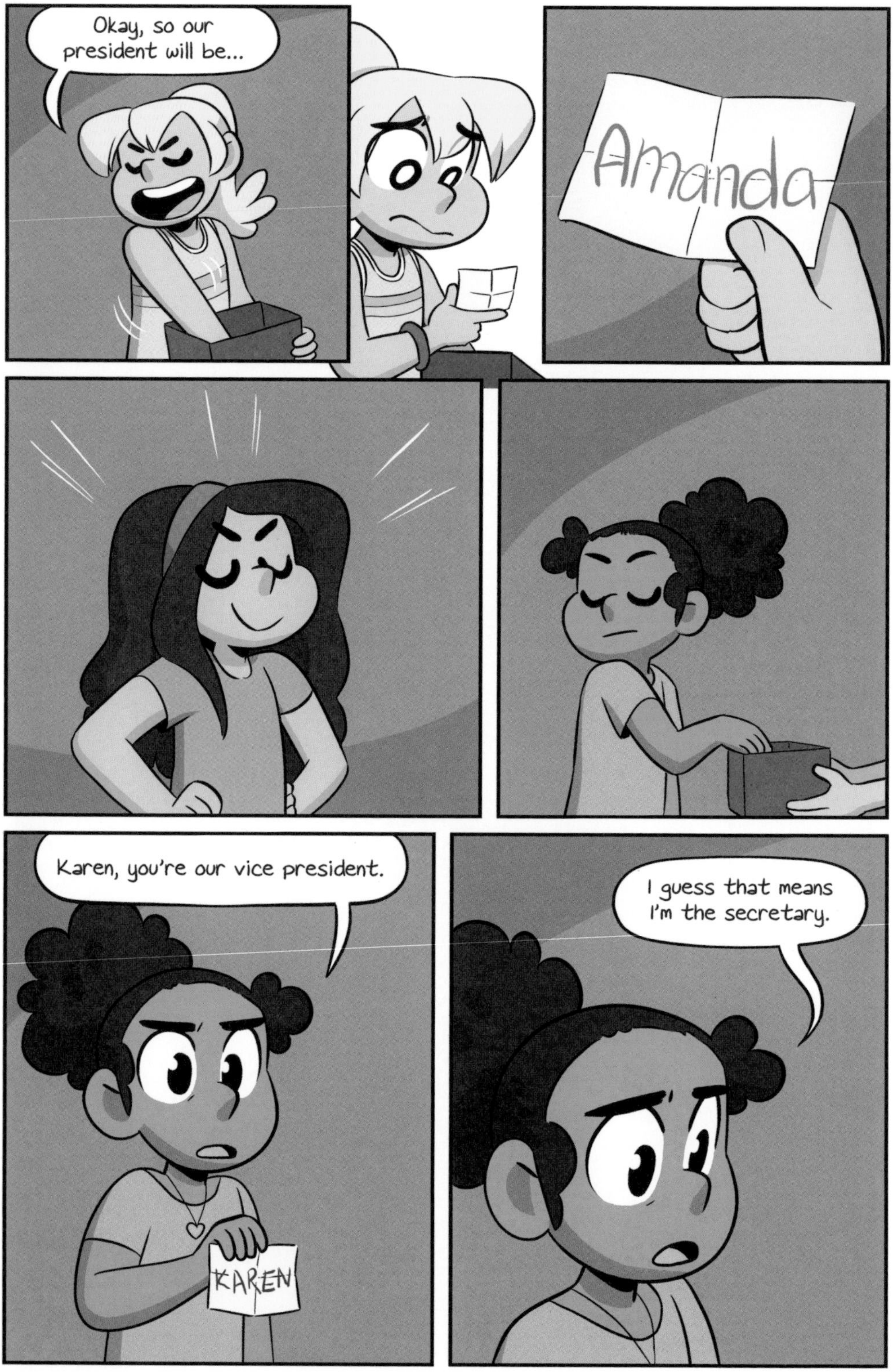
Okay, so our president will be...
Amanda
Karen, you're our vice president.
KAREN
I guess that means I'm the secretary.

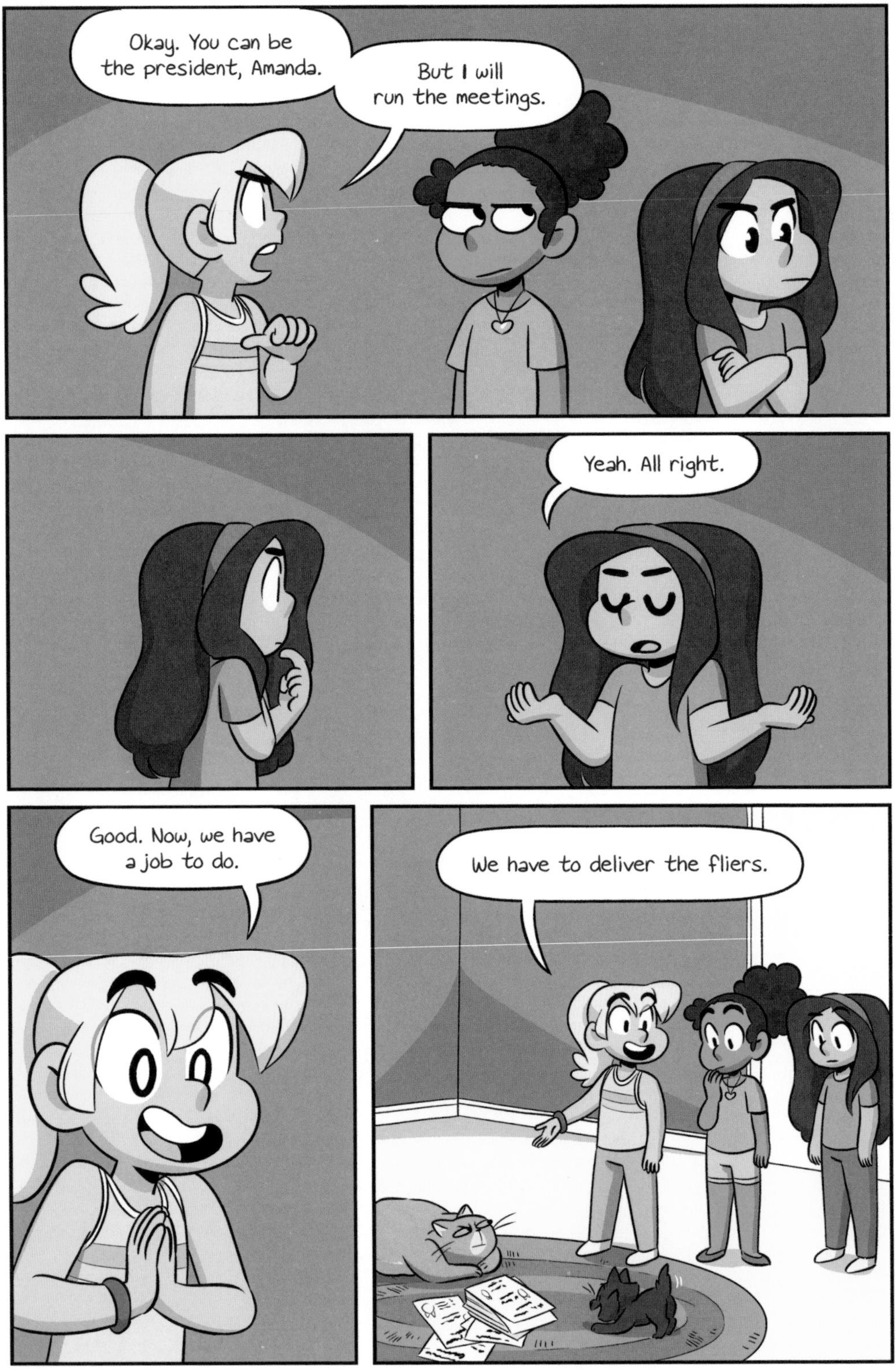
Okay. You can be the president, Amanda.
But I will run the meetings.
Yeah. All right.
Good. Now, we have a job to do.
We have to deliver the fliers.

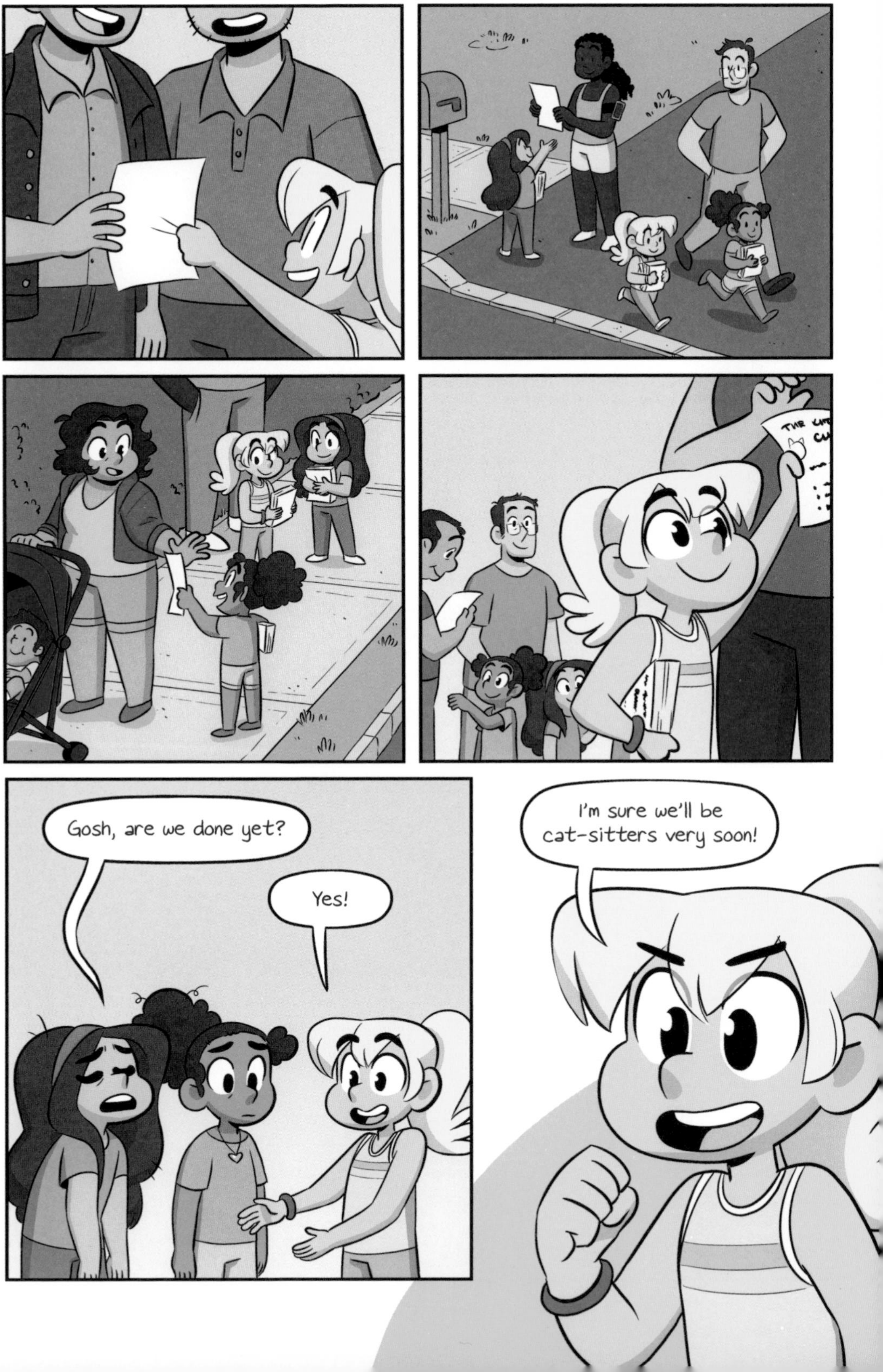
Gosh, are we done yet?
Yes!
I'm sure we'll be cat-sitters very soon!

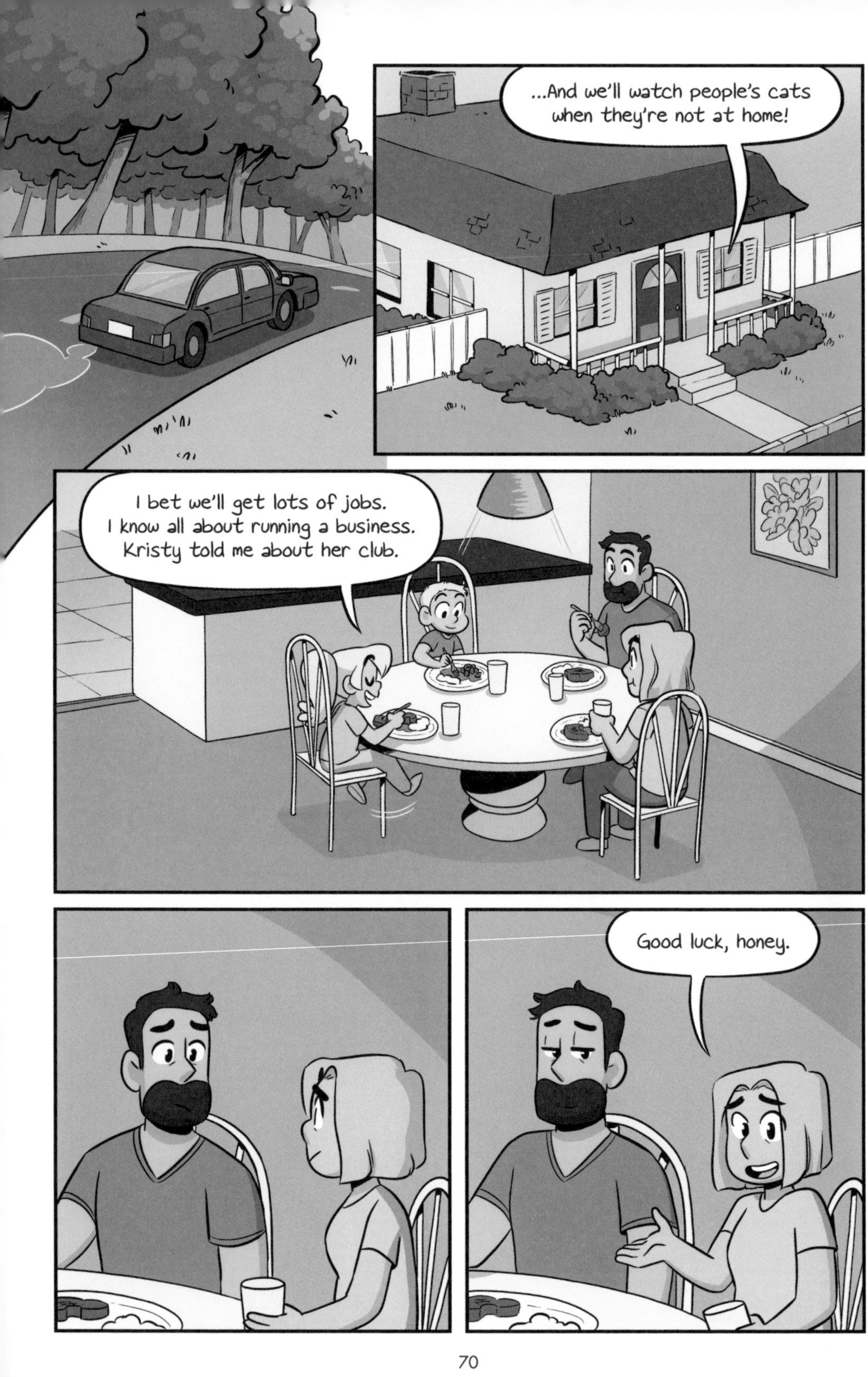
...And we'll watch people's cats when they're not at home!
I bet we'll get lots of jobs. I know all about running a business. Kristy told me about her club.
Good luck, honey.

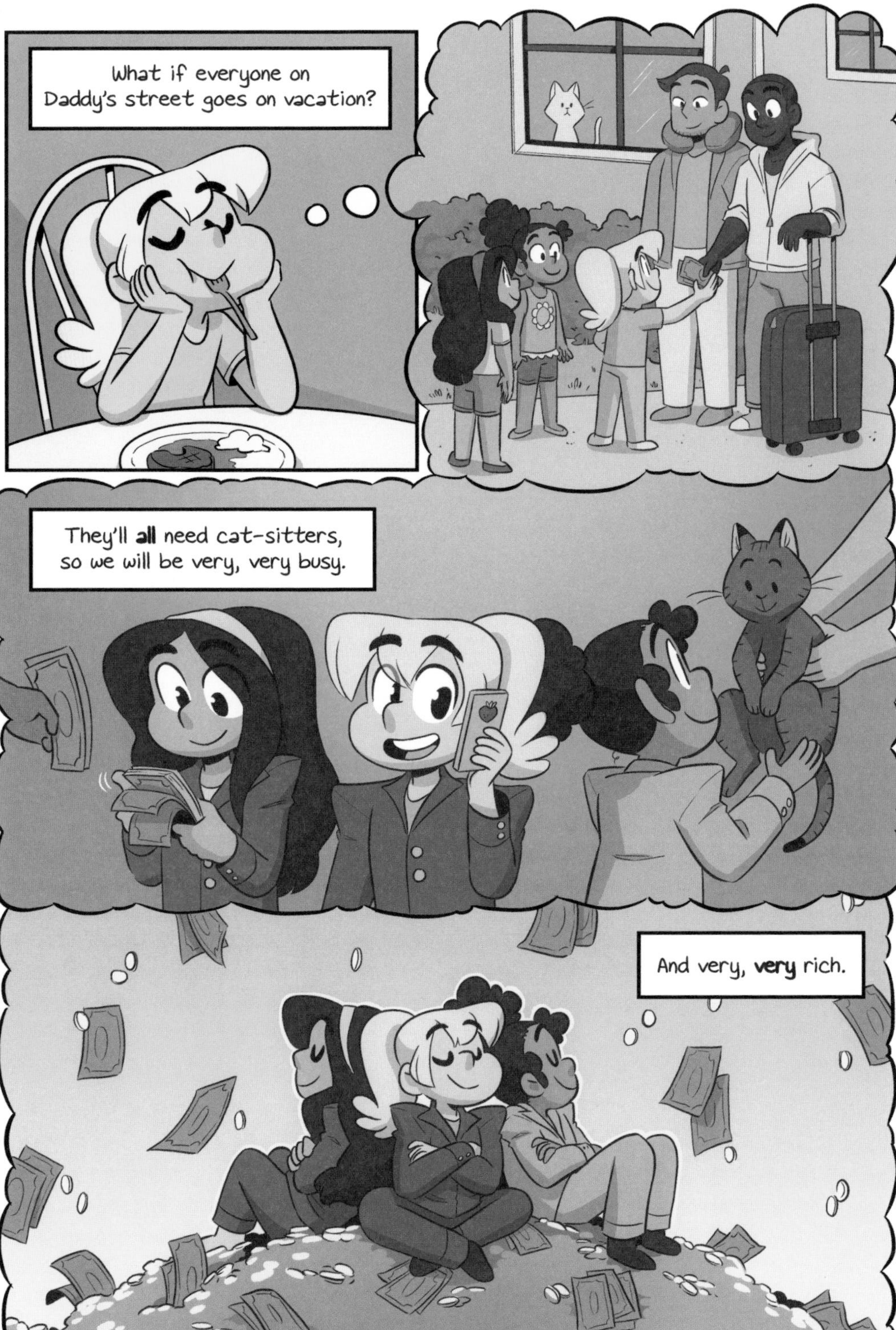
What if everyone on Daddy's street goes on vacation?
They'll **all** need cat-sitters, so we will be very, very busy.
And very, **very** rich.

CHAPTER 6

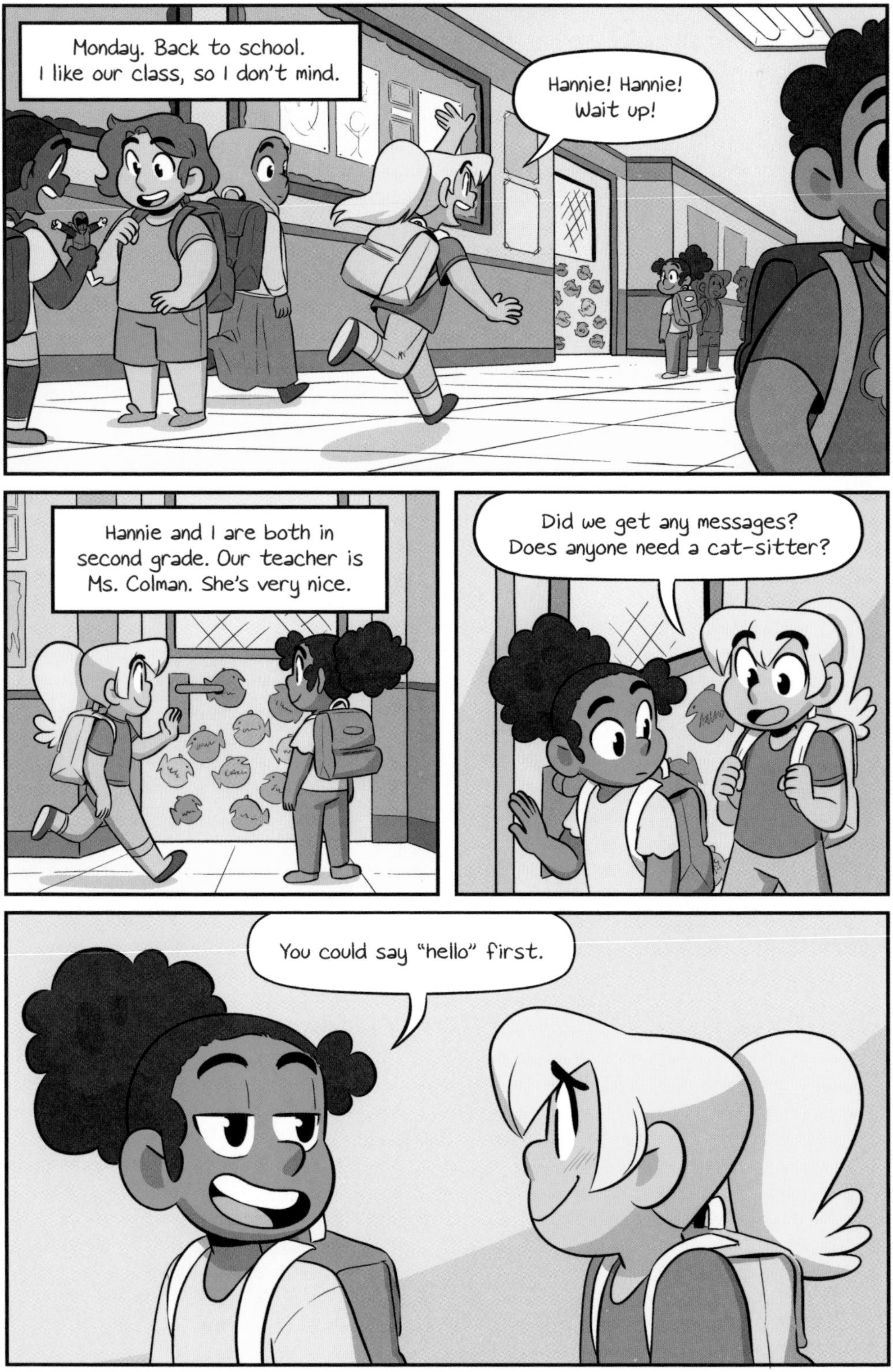
Monday. Back to school. I like our class, so I don't mind.
Hannie! Hannie! Wait up!
Hannie and I are both in second grade. Our teacher is Ms. Colman. She's very nice.
Did we get any messages? Does anyone need a cat-sitter?
You could say "hello" first.

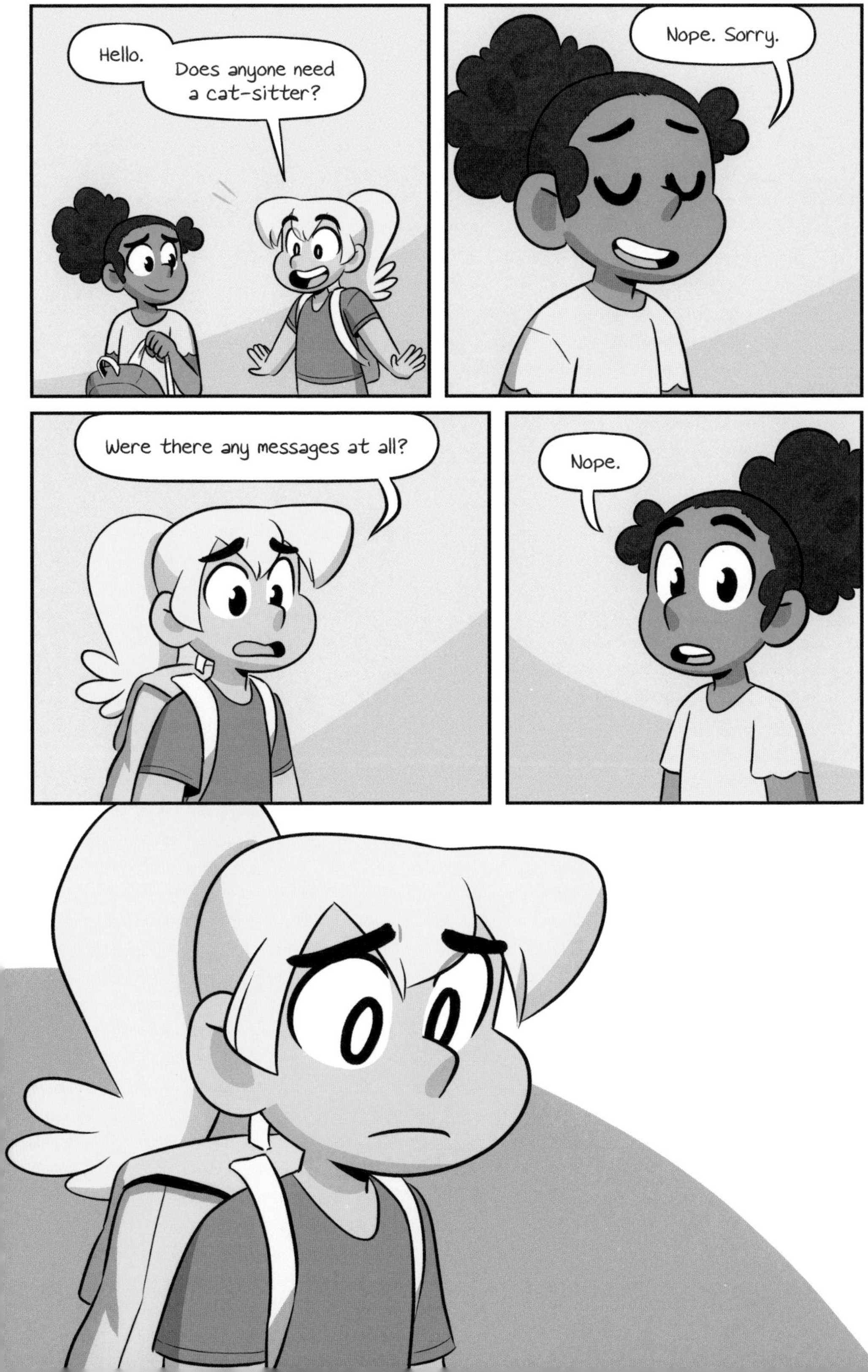
Hello.
Does anyone need a cat-sitter?
Nope. Sorry.
Were there any messages at all?
Nope.

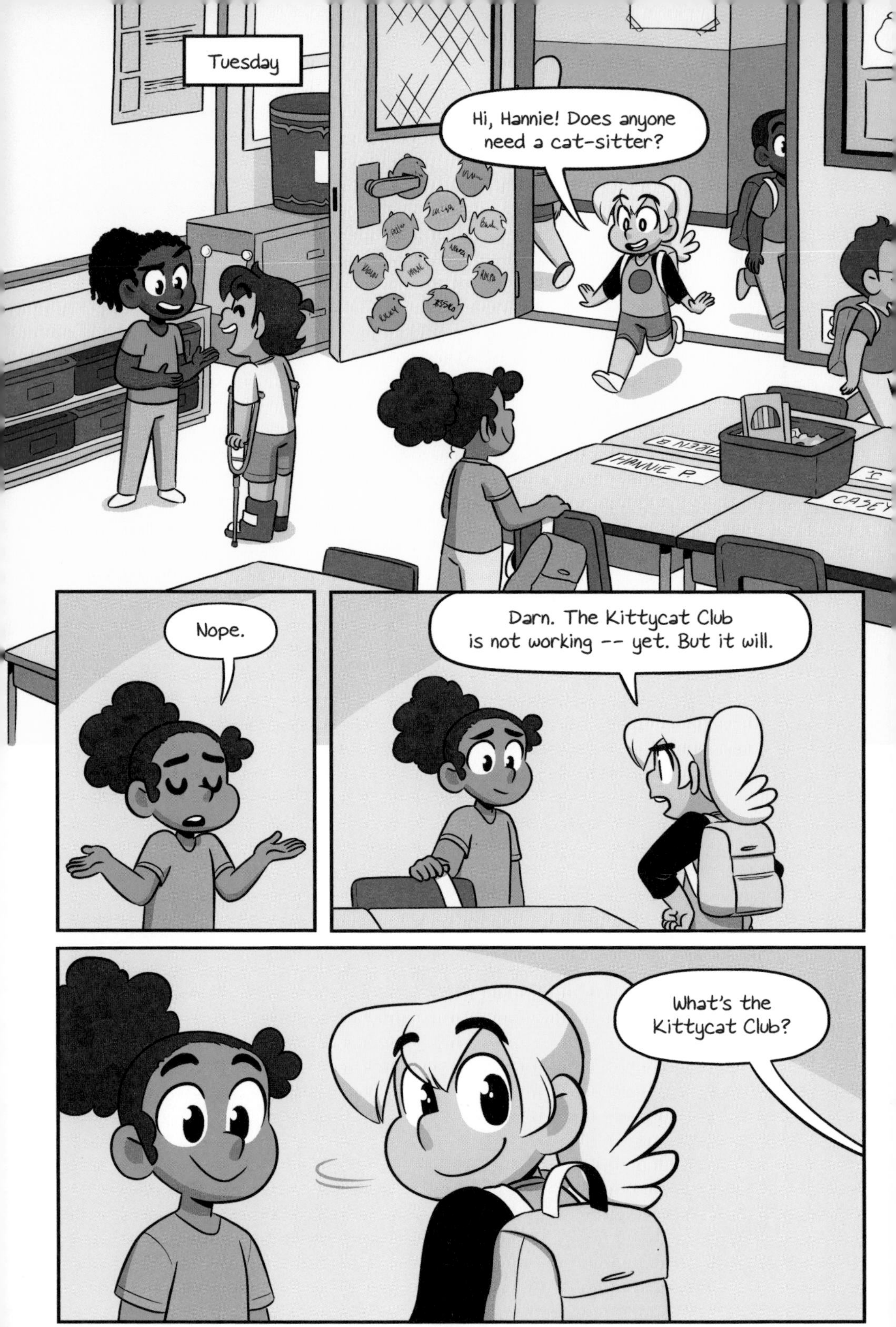
Tuesday
Hi, Hannie! Does anyone need a cat-sitter?
HANNIE P.
CASEY
Nope.
Darn. The Kittycat Club is not working -- yet. But it will.
What's the Kittycat Club?

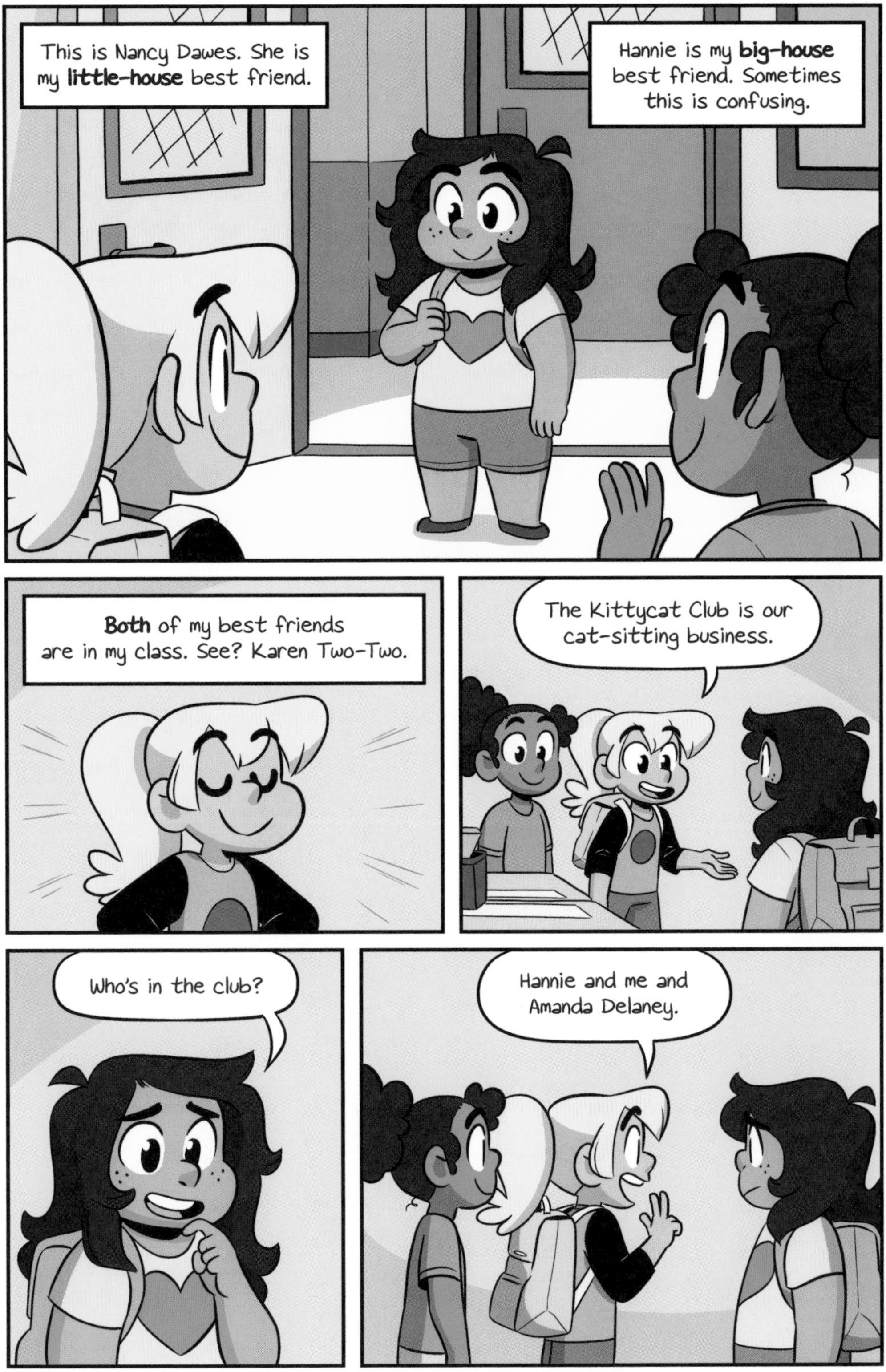
This is Nancy Dawes. She is my **little-house** best friend.
Hannie is my **big-house** best friend. Sometimes this is confusing.
Both of my best friends are in my class. See? Karen Two-Two.
The Kittycat Club is our cat-sitting business.
Who's in the club?
Hannie and me and Amanda Delaney.

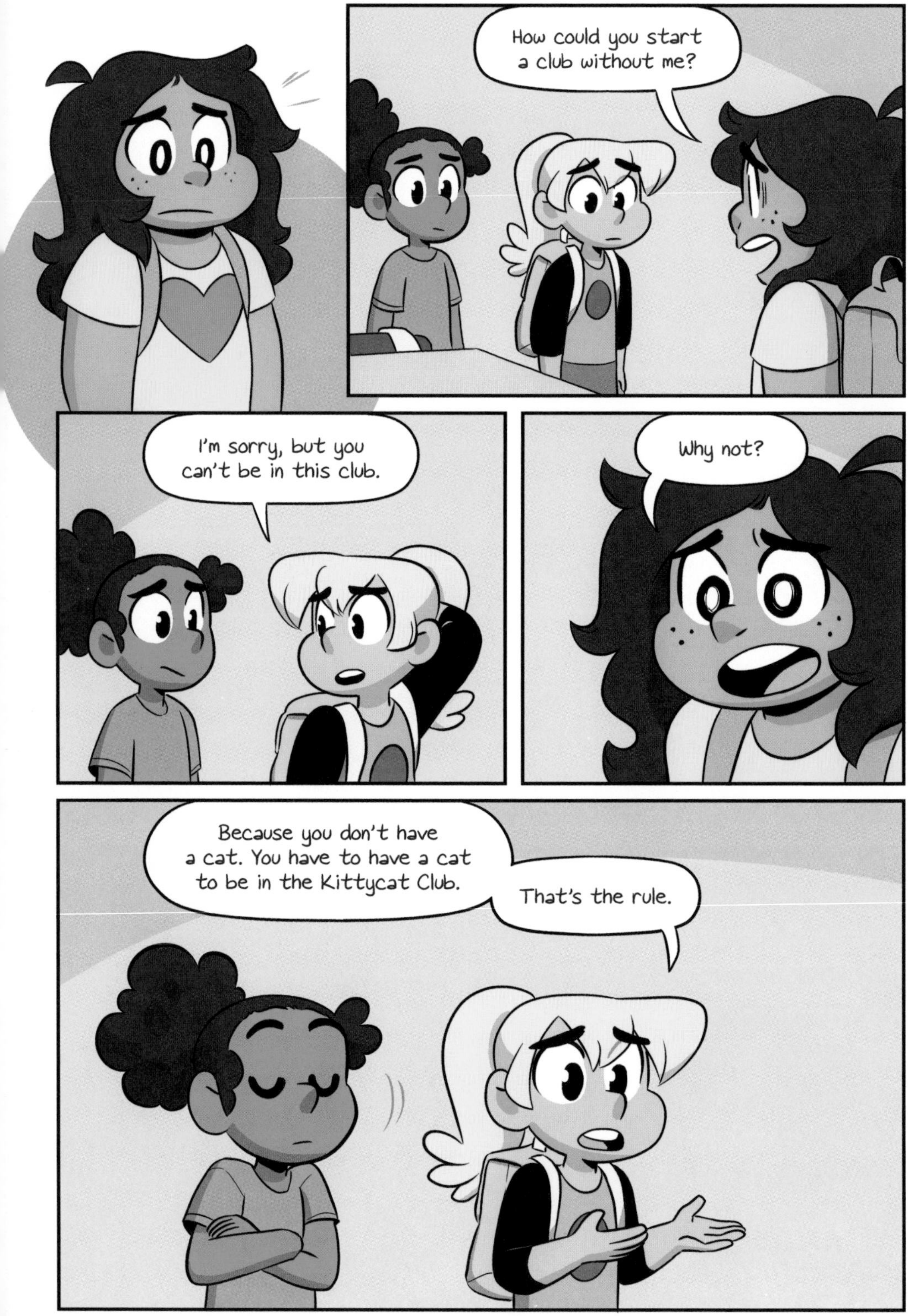
How could you start a club without me?
I'm sorry, but you can't be in this club.
Why not?
Because you don't have a cat. You have to have a cat to be in the Kittycat Club.
That's the rule.

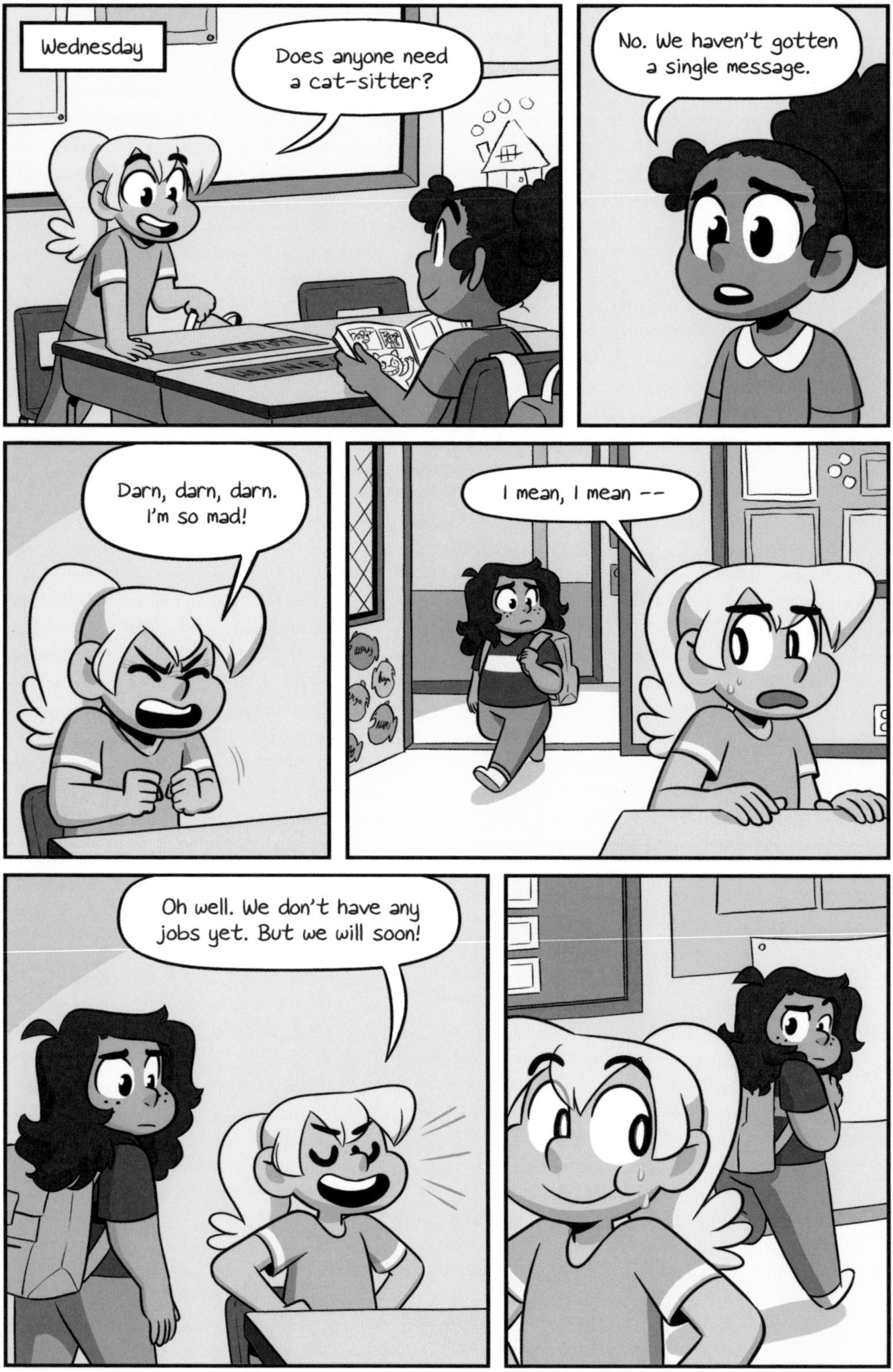
Wednesday
Does anyone need a cat-sitter?
No. We haven't gotten a single message.
Darn, darn, darn. I'm so mad!
I mean, I mean --
Oh well. We don't have any jobs yet. But we will soon!

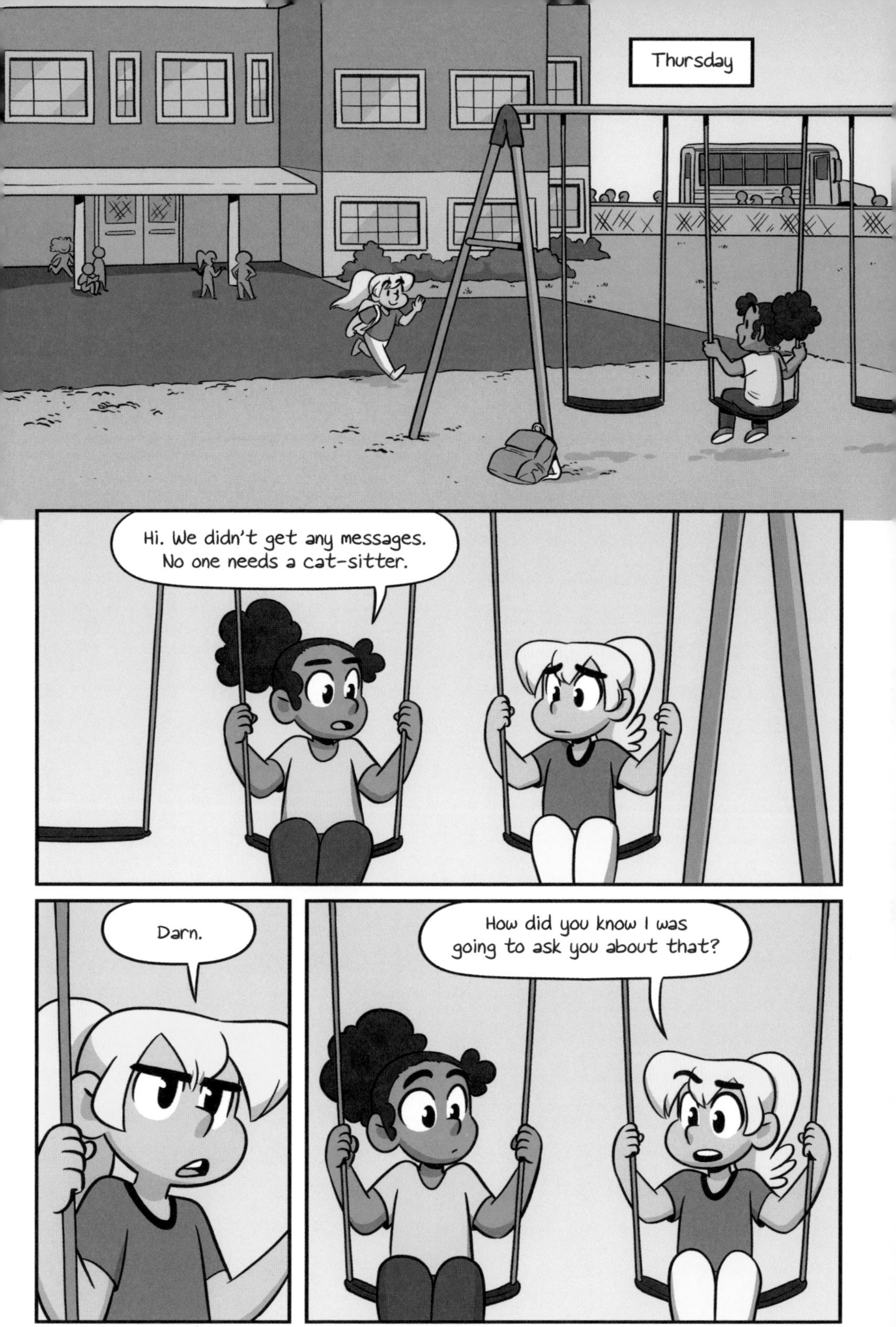
Thursday
Hi. We didn't get any messages. No one needs a cat-sitter.
Darn.
How did you know I was going to ask you about that?

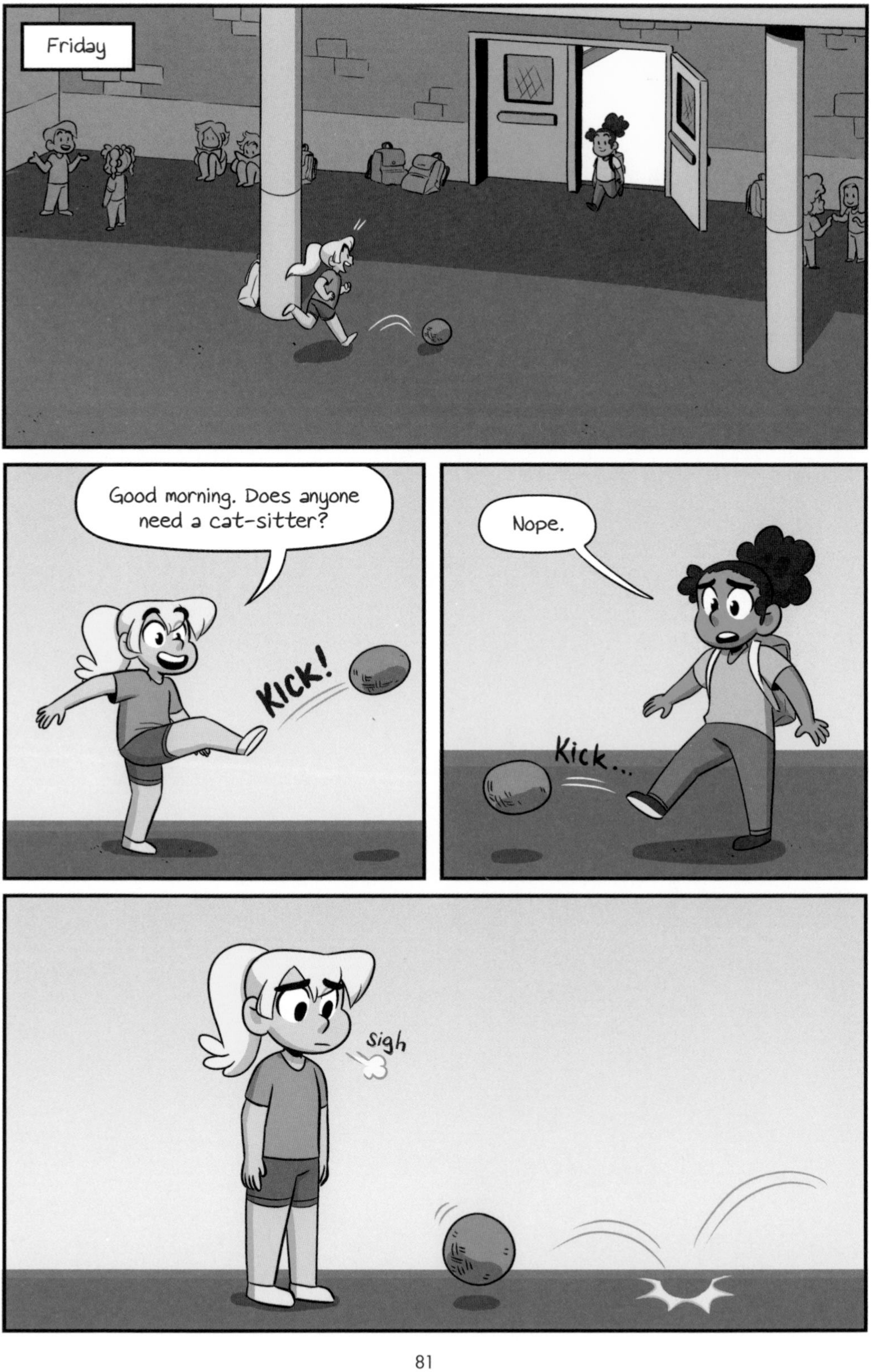
Friday
Good morning. Does anyone need a cat-sitter?
KICK!
Nope.
Kick...
sigh

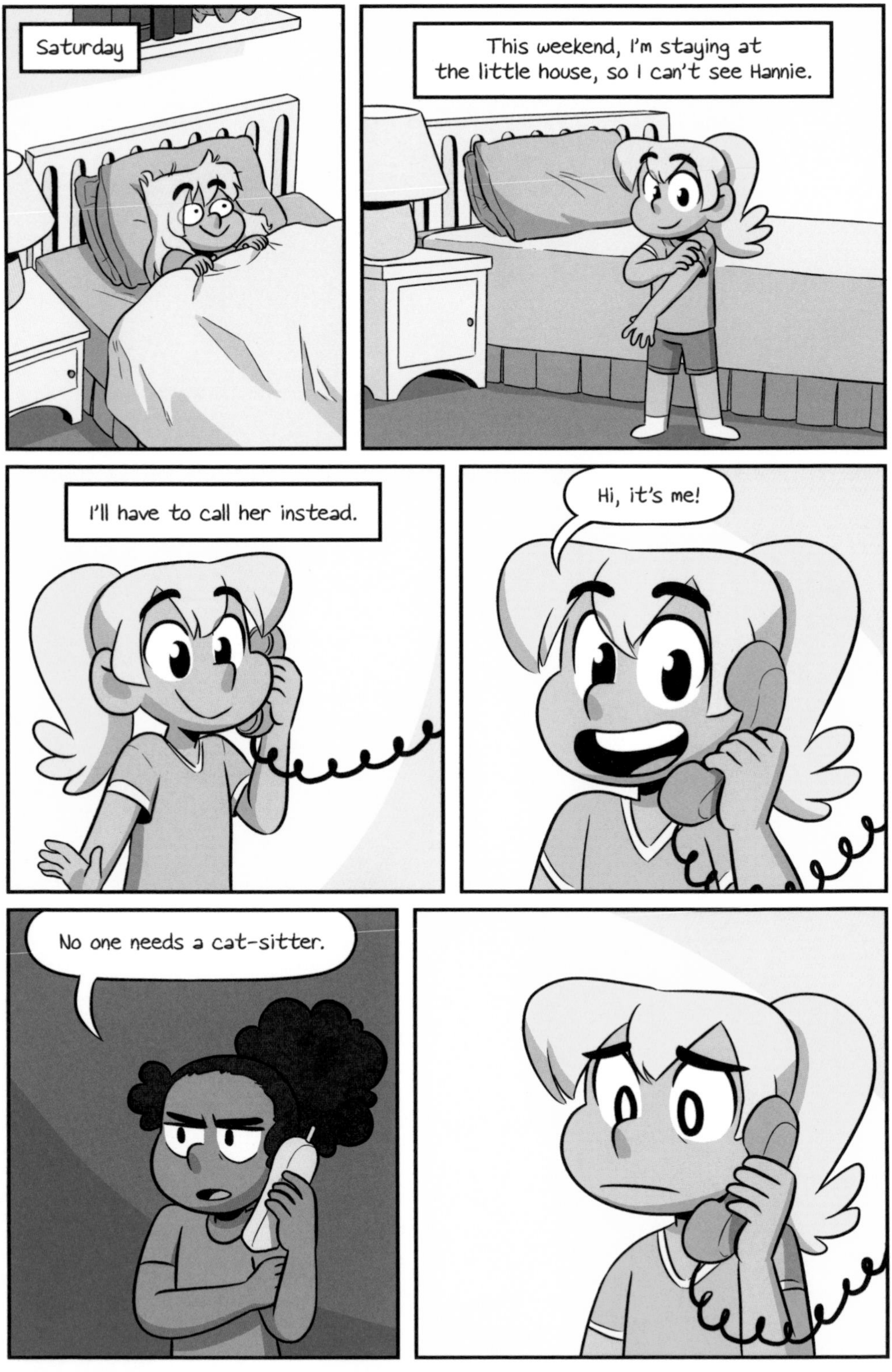
Saturday
This weekend, I'm staying at the little house, so I can't see Hannie.
I'll have to call her instead.
Hi, it's me!
No one needs a cat-sitter.

CHAPTER 7

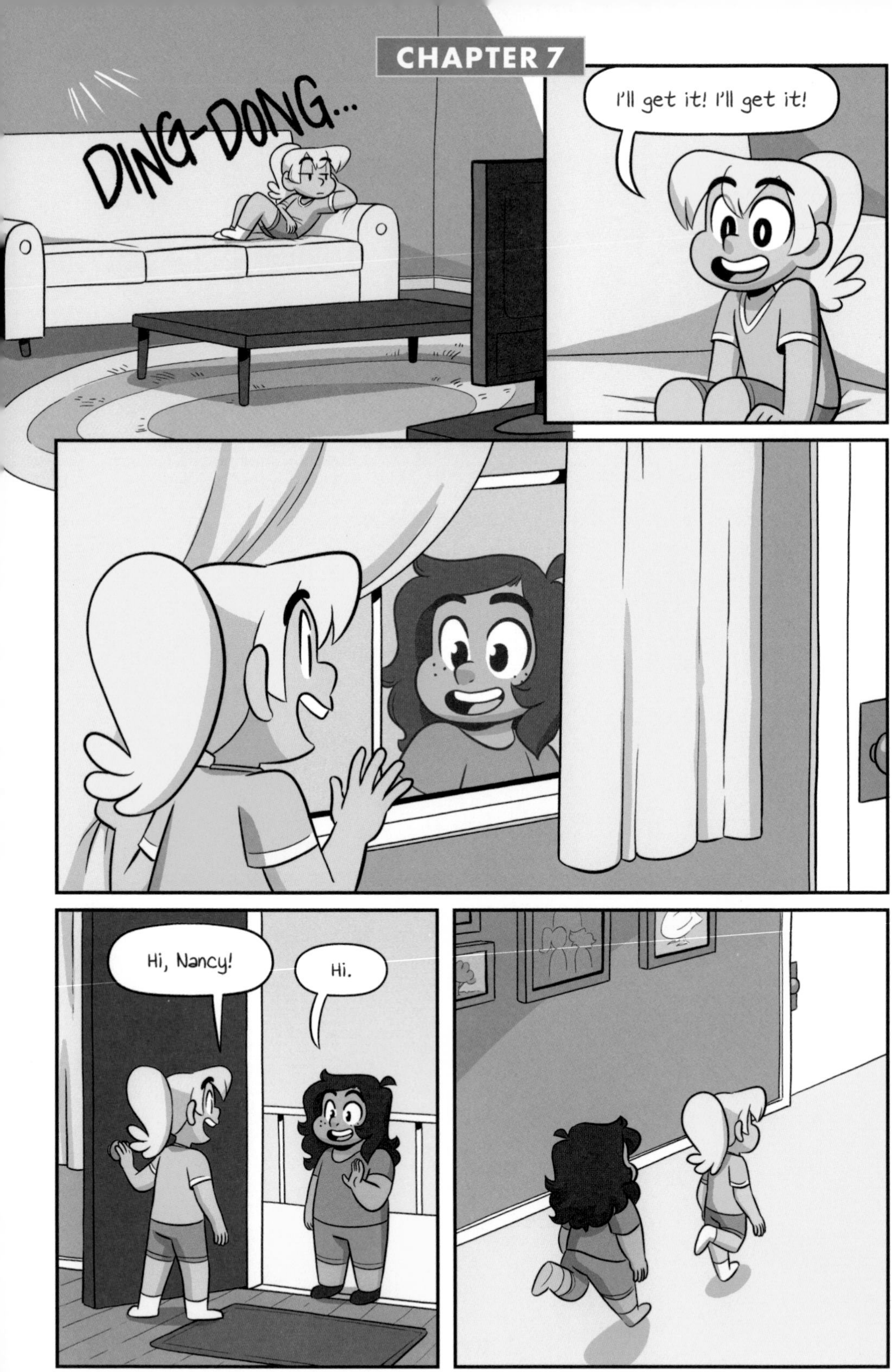

DING-DONG...
I'll get it! I'll get it!
Hi, Nancy!
Hi.

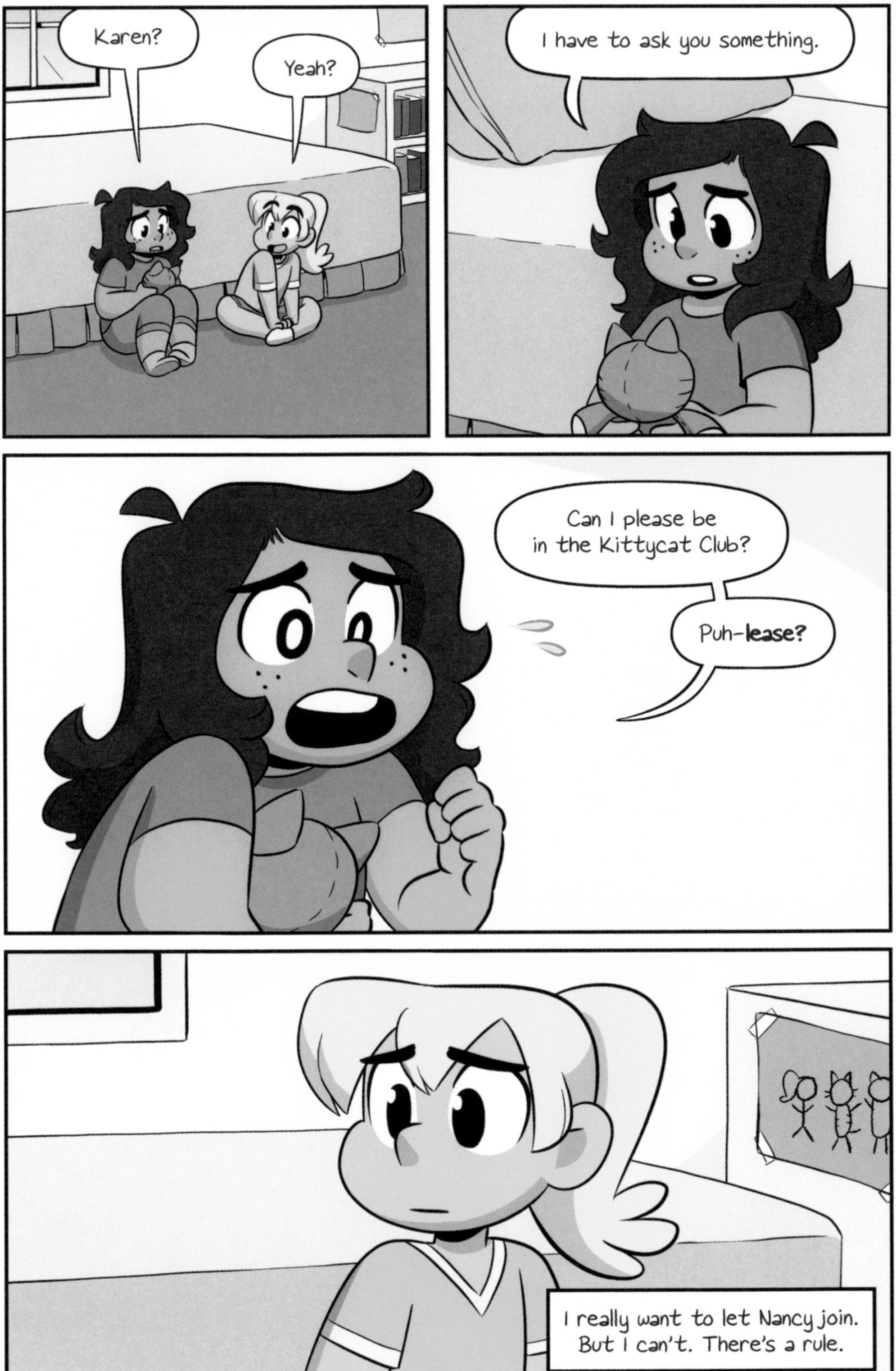
Karen?
Yeah?
I have to ask you something.
Can I please be in the Kittycat Club?
Puh-**lease?**
I really want to let Nancy join. But I can't. There's a rule.

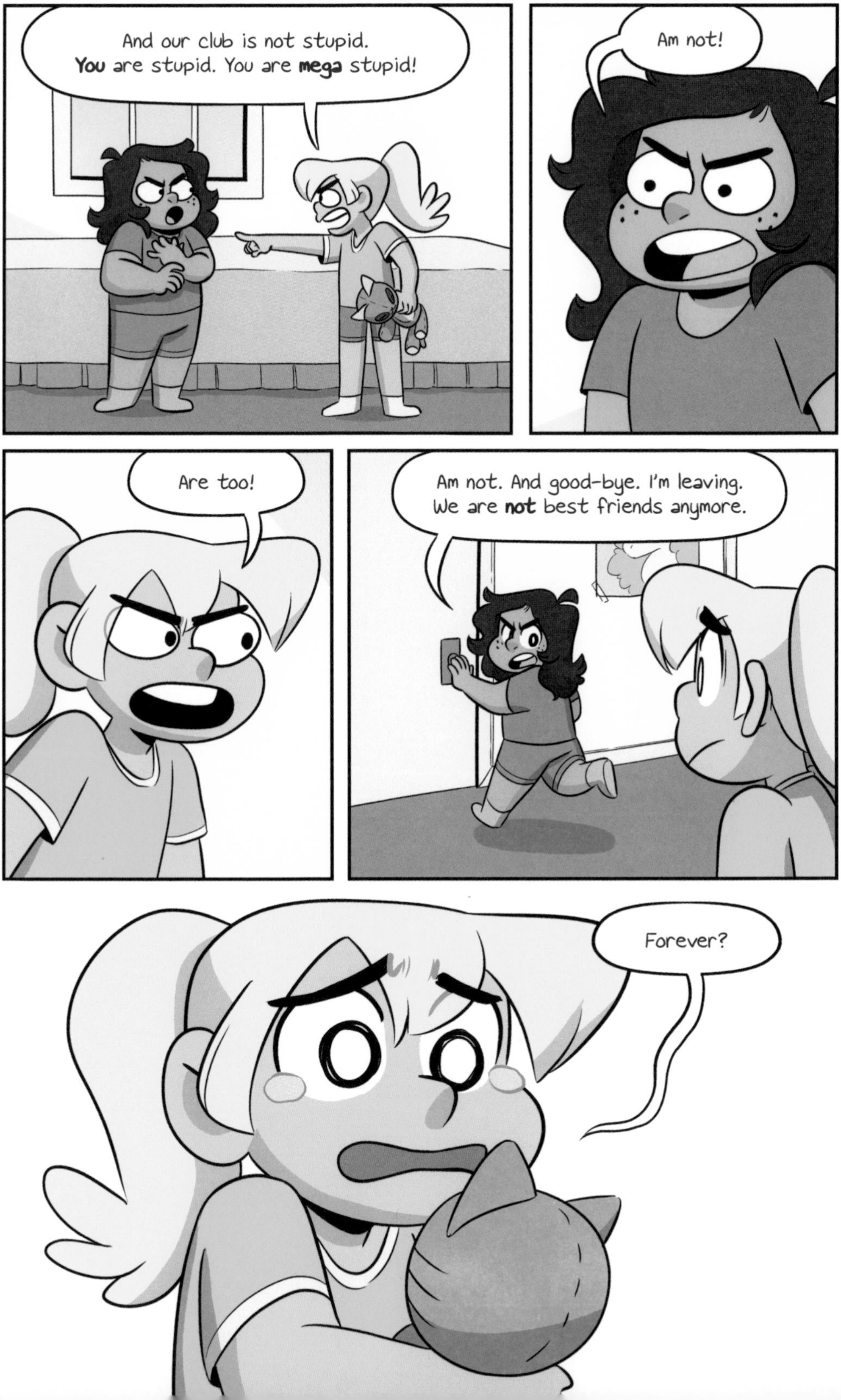
And our club is not stupid.
You are stupid. You are **mega** stupid!
Am not!
Are too!
Am not. And good-bye. I'm leaving.
We are **not** best friends anymore.
Forever?

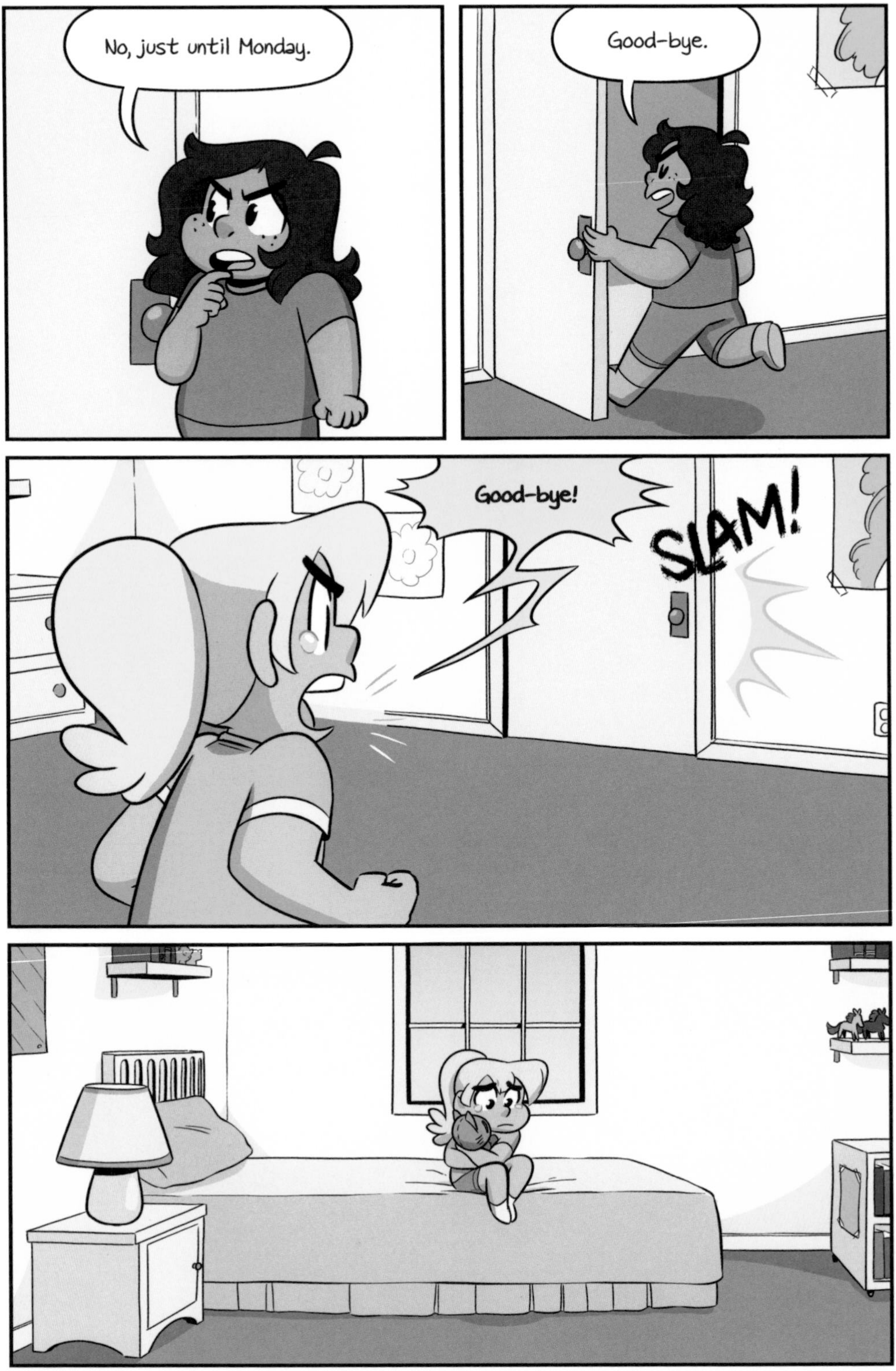
No, just until Monday.
Good-bye.
Good-bye!
SLAM!

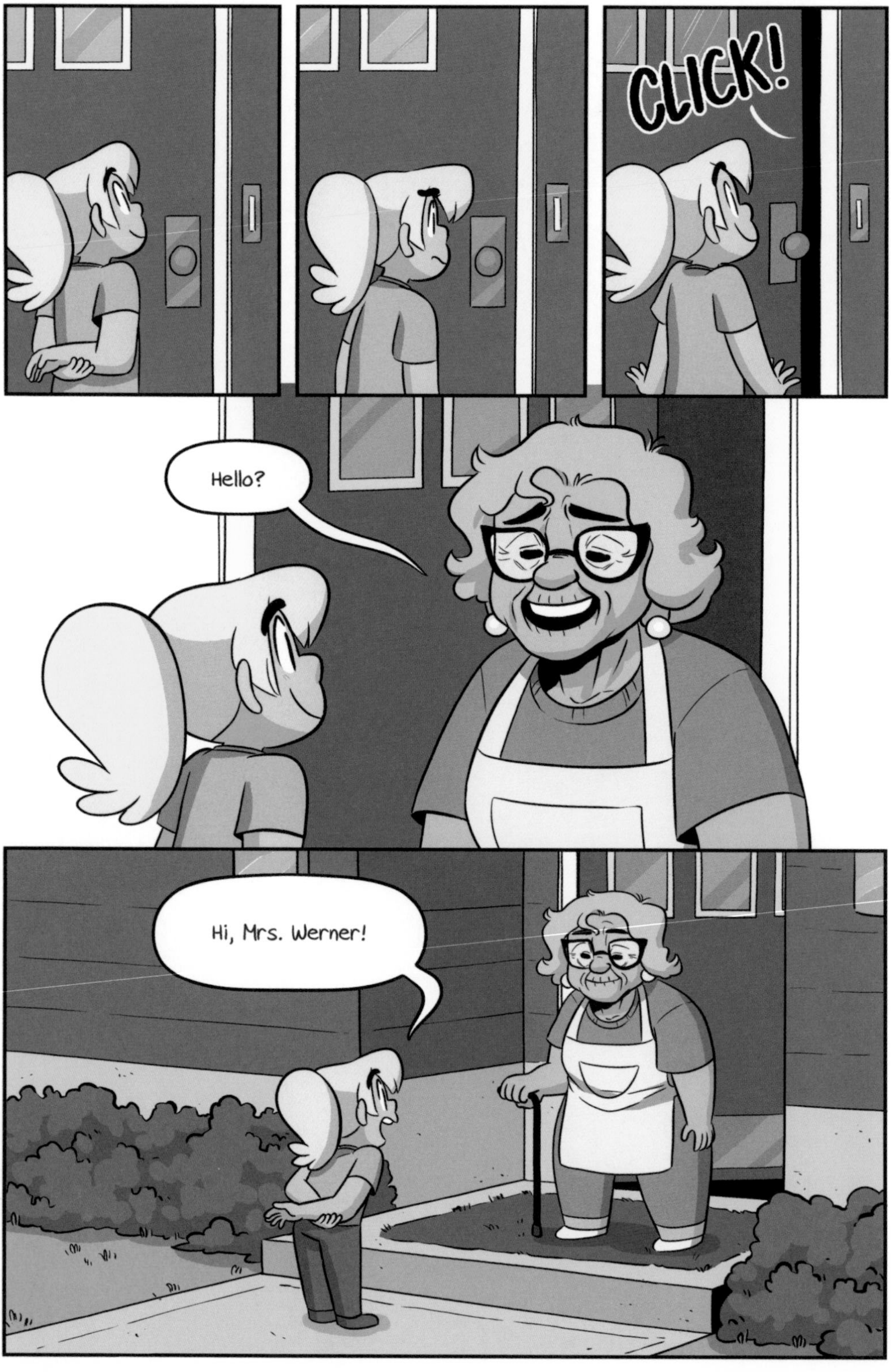
CLICK!
Hello?
Hi, Mrs. Werner!

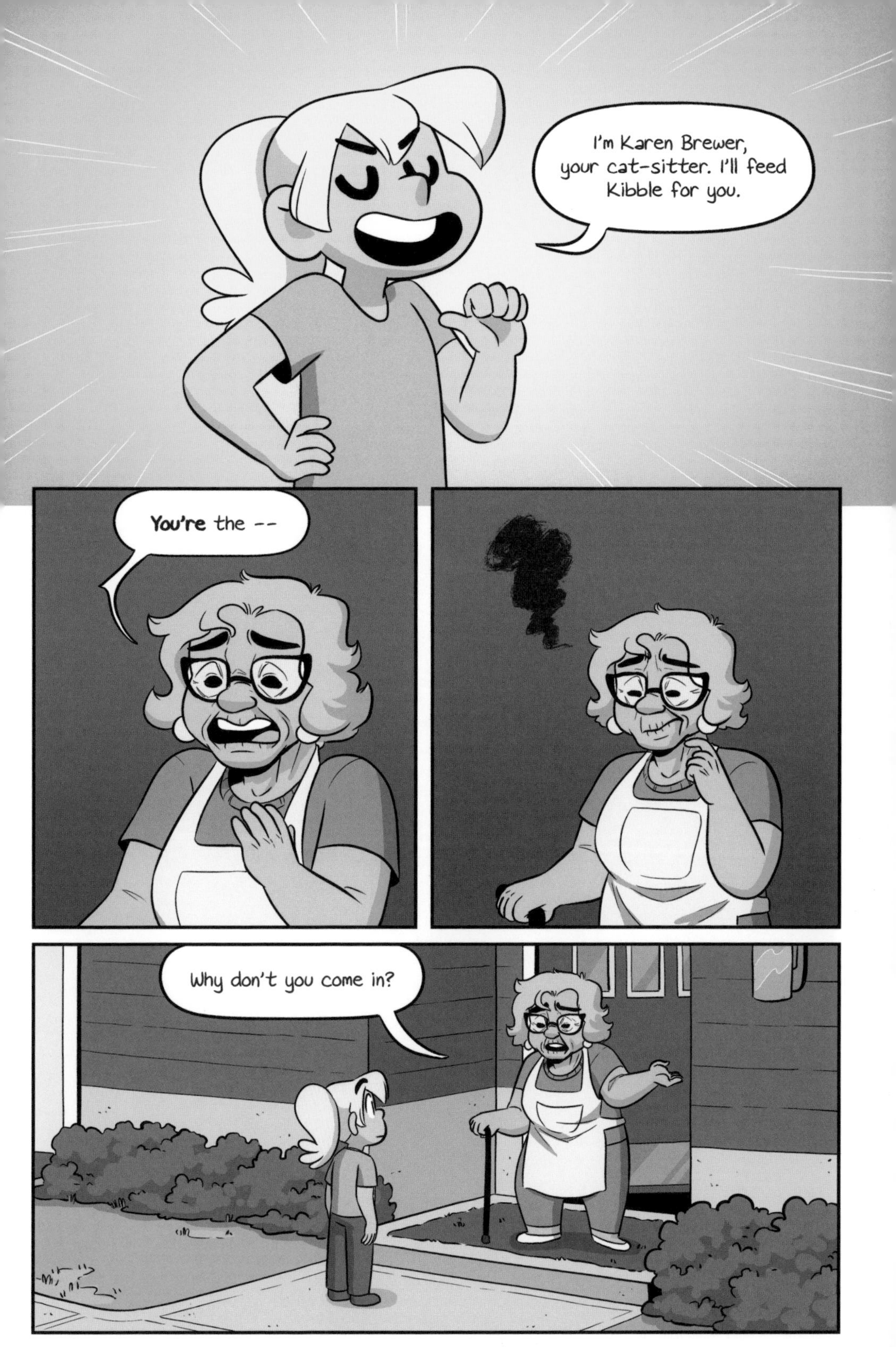
I'm Karen Brewer, your cat-sitter. I'll feed Kibble for you.
You're the --
Why don't you come in?

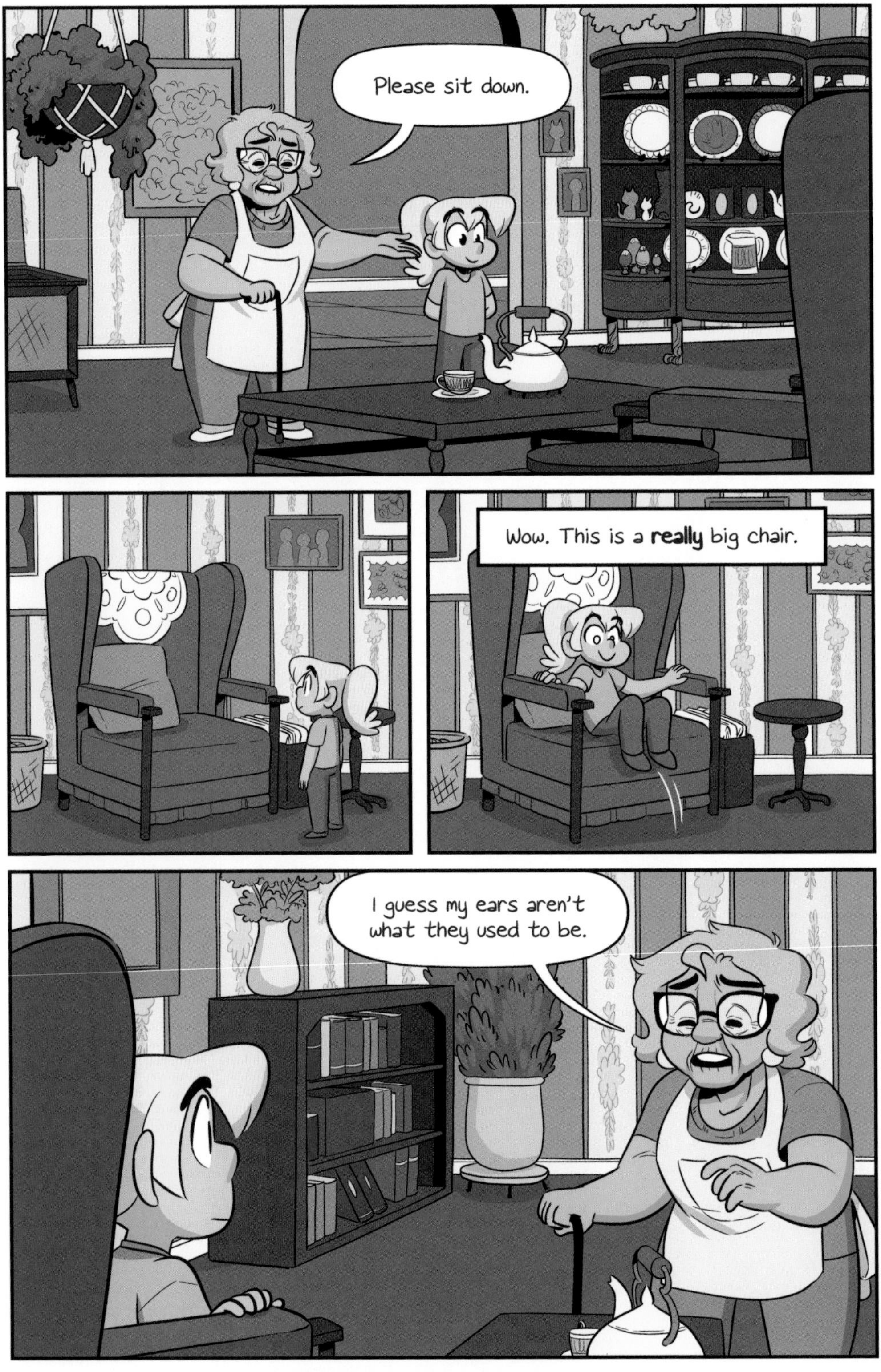
Please sit down.
Wow. This is a **really** big chair.
I guess my ears aren't what they used to be.

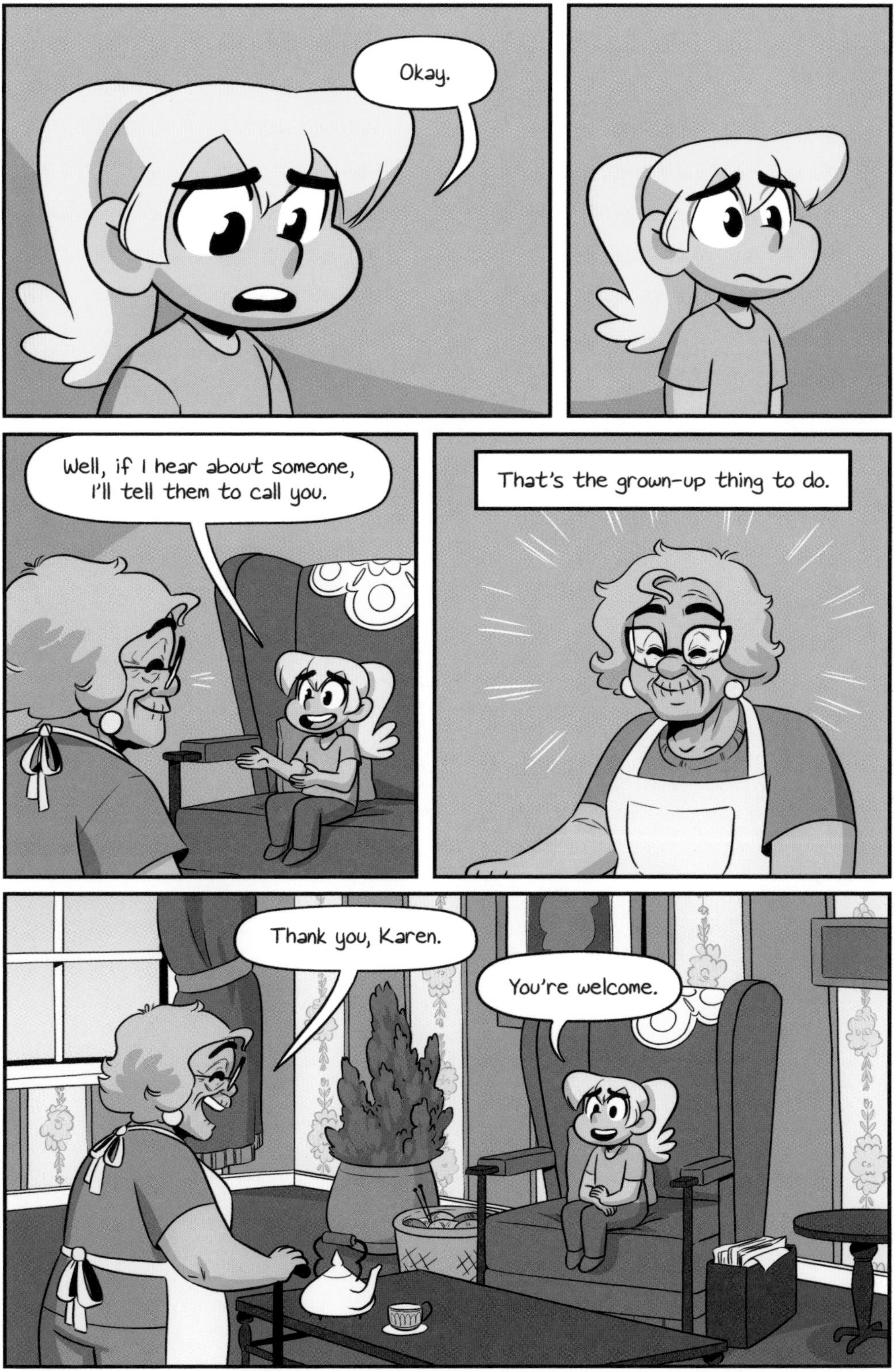
Okay.
Well, if I hear about someone, I'll tell them to call you.
That's the grown-up thing to do.
Thank you, Karen.
You're welcome.

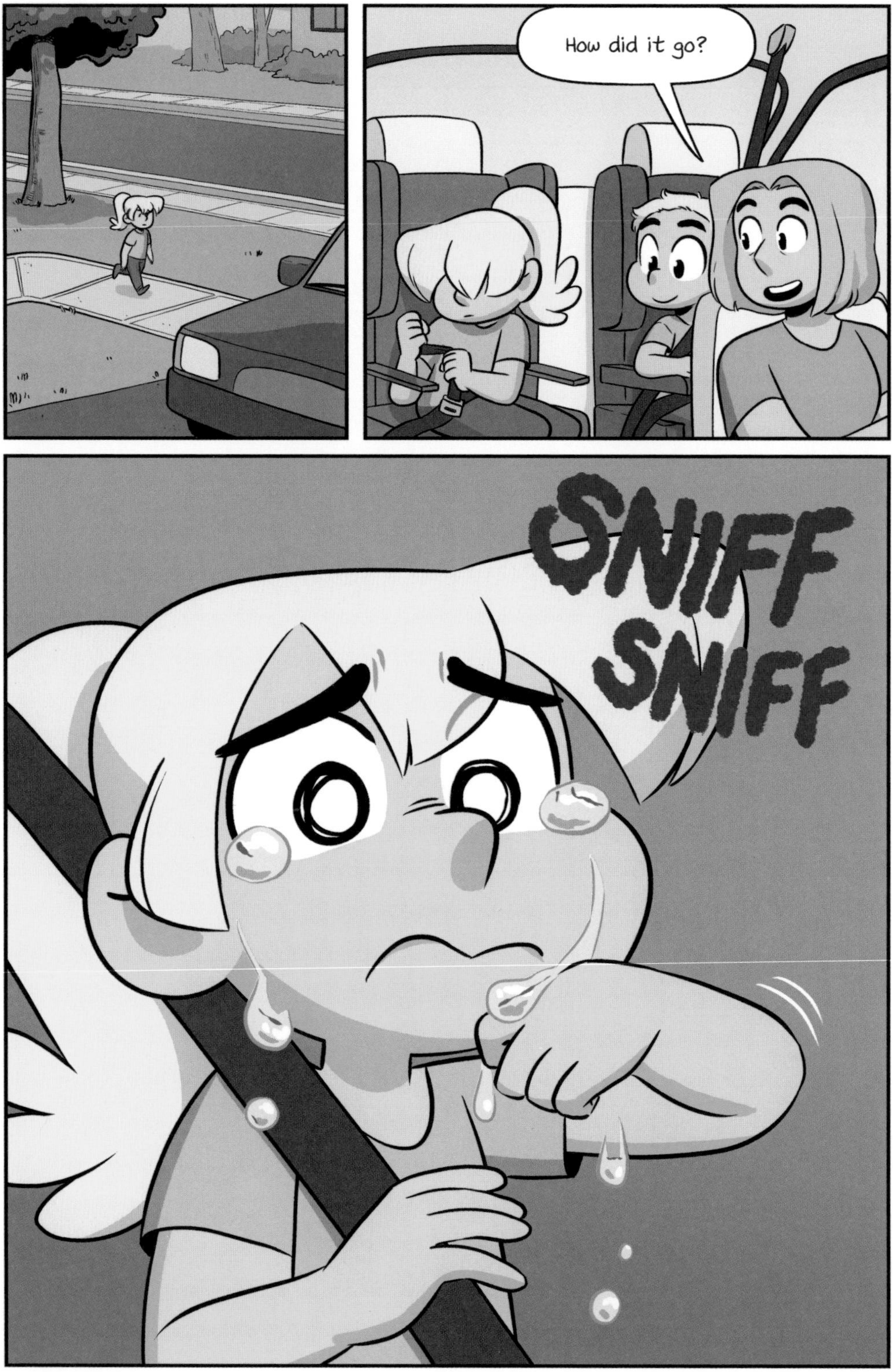
How did it go?
SNIFF
SNIFF

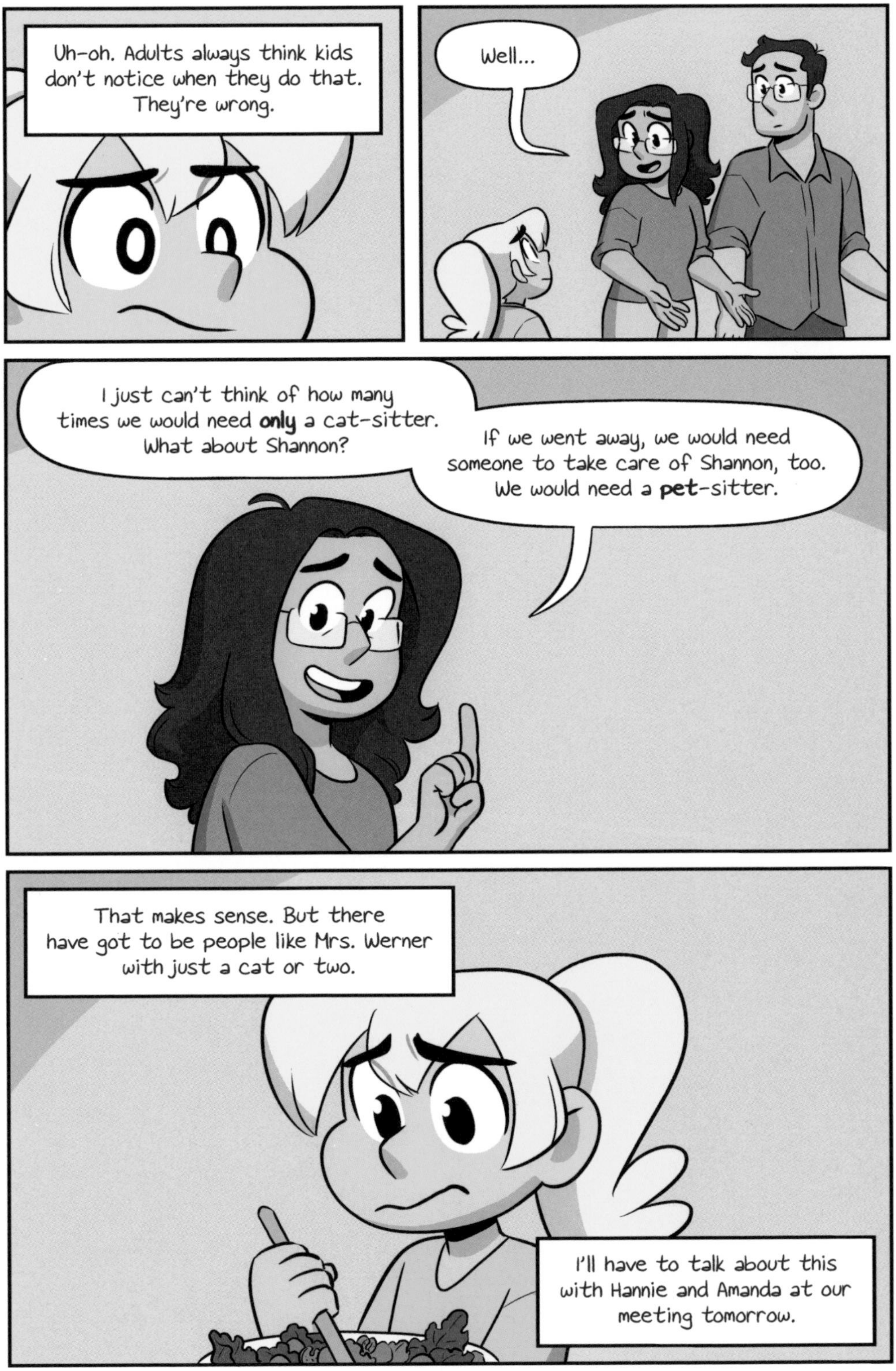
Uh-oh. Adults always think kids don't notice when they do that. They're wrong.
Well...
I just can't think of how many times we would need **only** a cat-sitter. What about Shannon?
If we went away, we would need someone to take care of Shannon, too. We would need a **pet**-sitter.
That makes sense. But there have got to be people like Mrs. Werner with just a cat or two.
I'll have to talk about this with Hannie and Amanda at our meeting tomorrow.

111

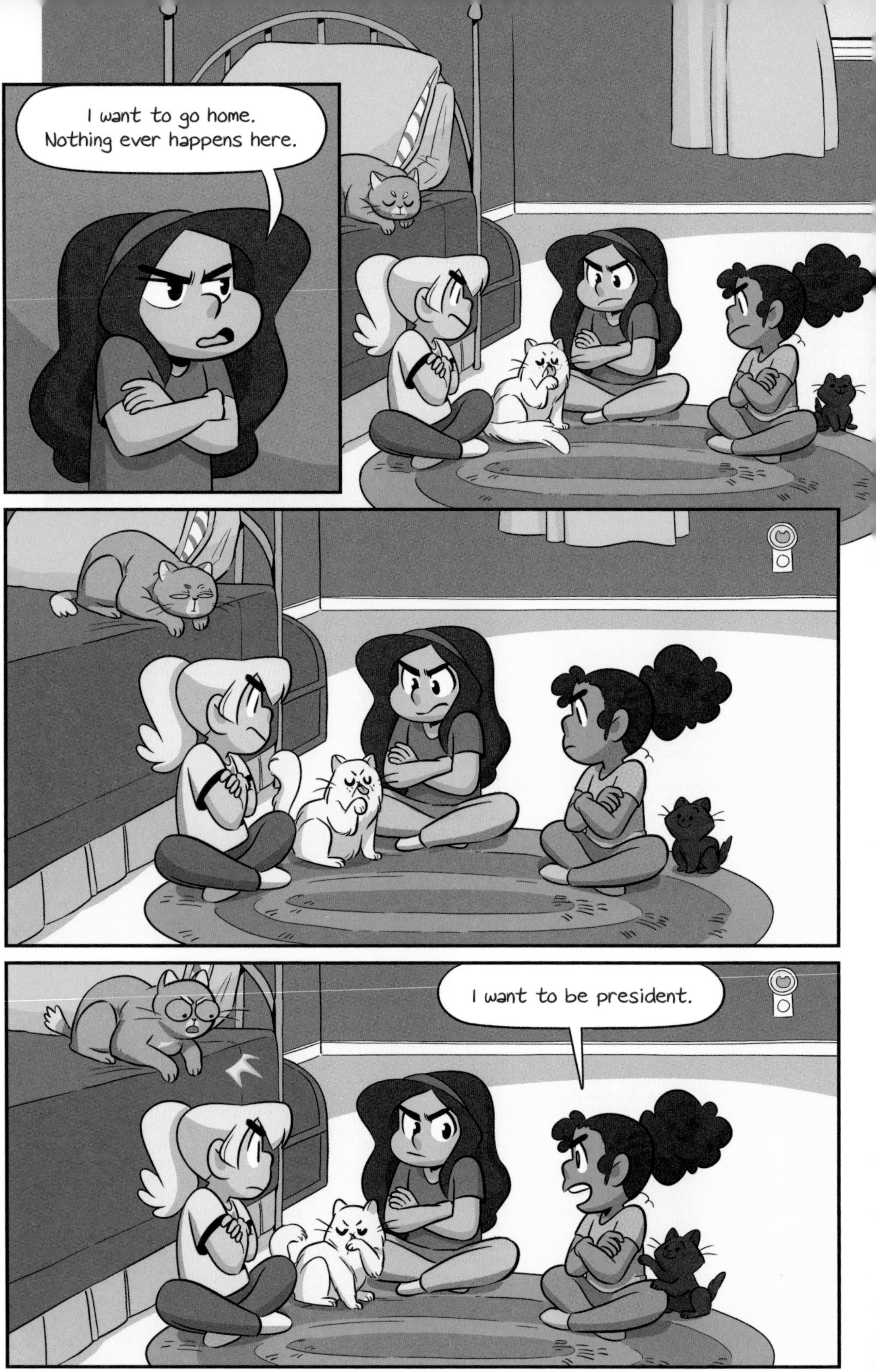
I want to go home.
Nothing ever happens here.
I want to be president.

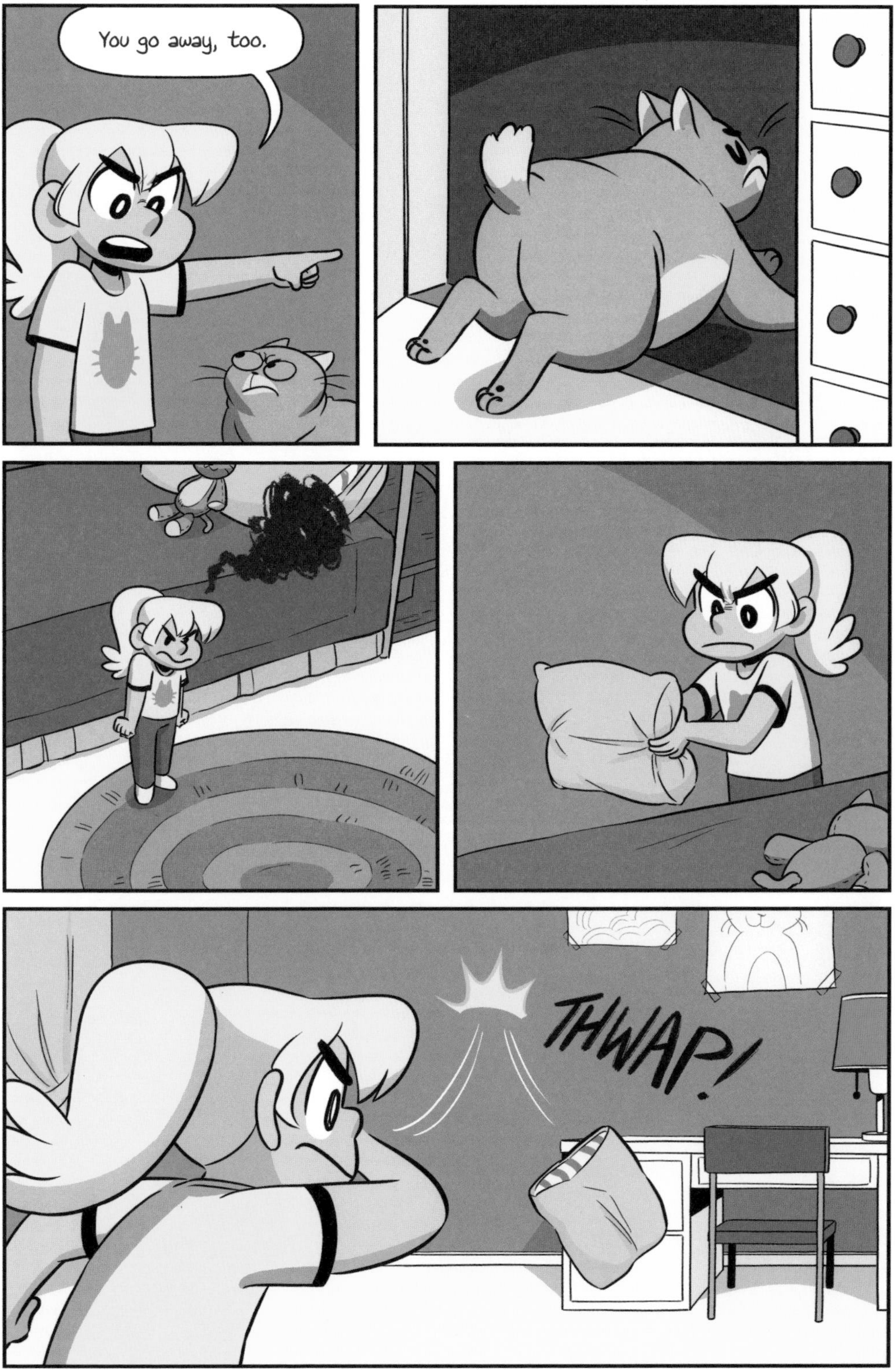

You go away, too.
THWAP!

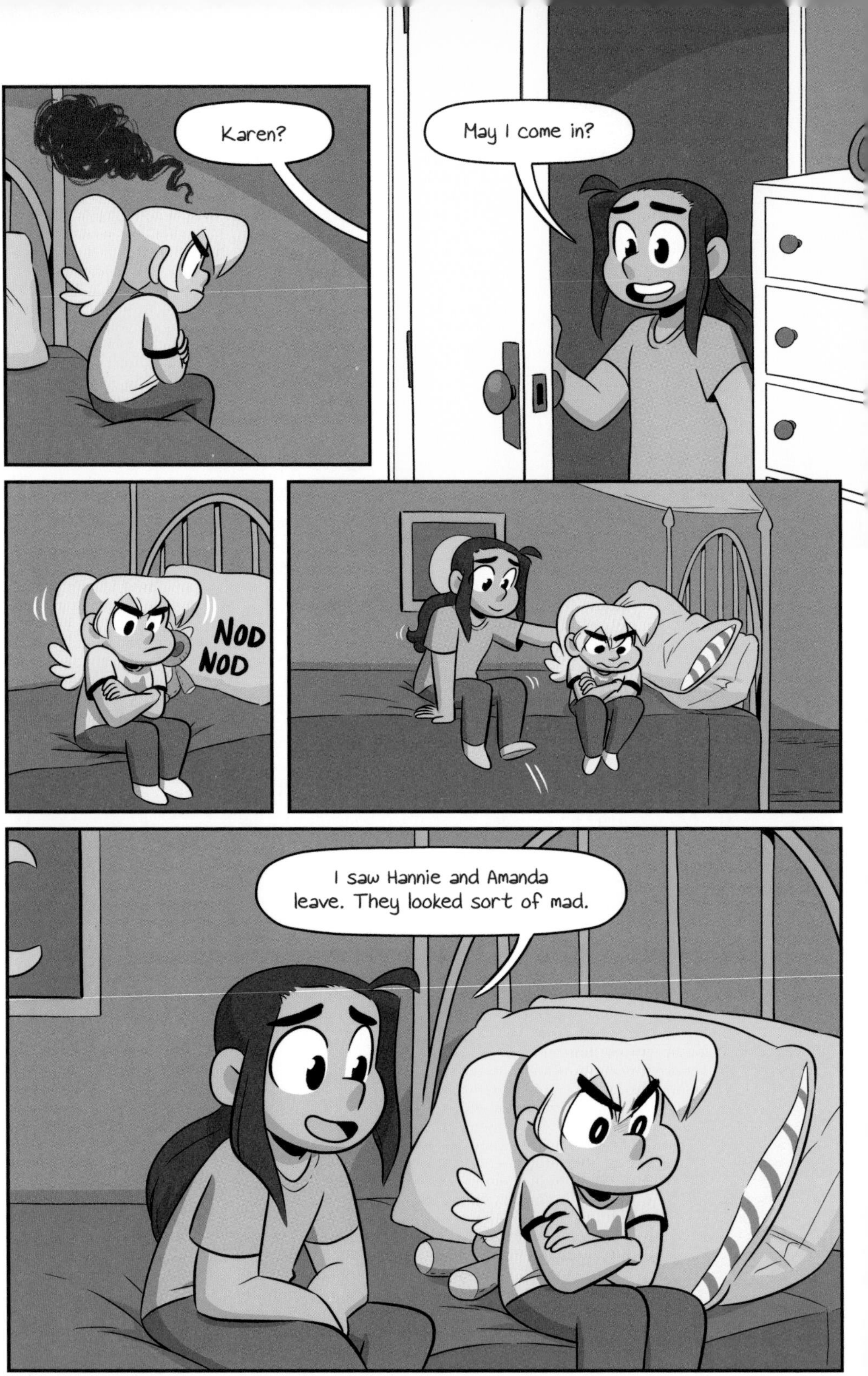
Karen?
May I come in?
NOD NOD
I saw Hannie and Amanda leave. They looked sort of mad.

124

127

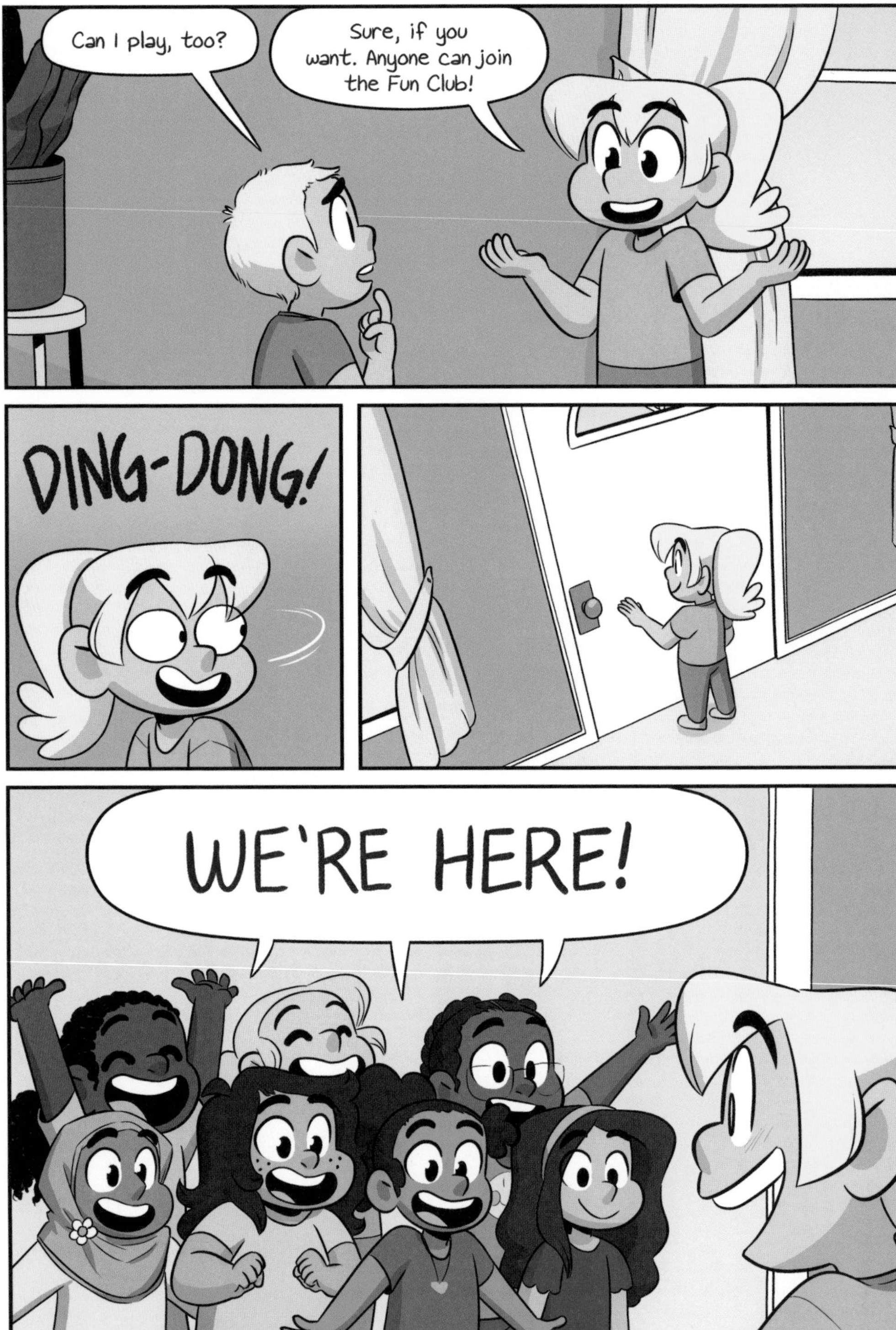
Can I play, too?
Sure, if you want. Anyone can join the Fun Club!
DING-DONG!
WE'RE HERE!

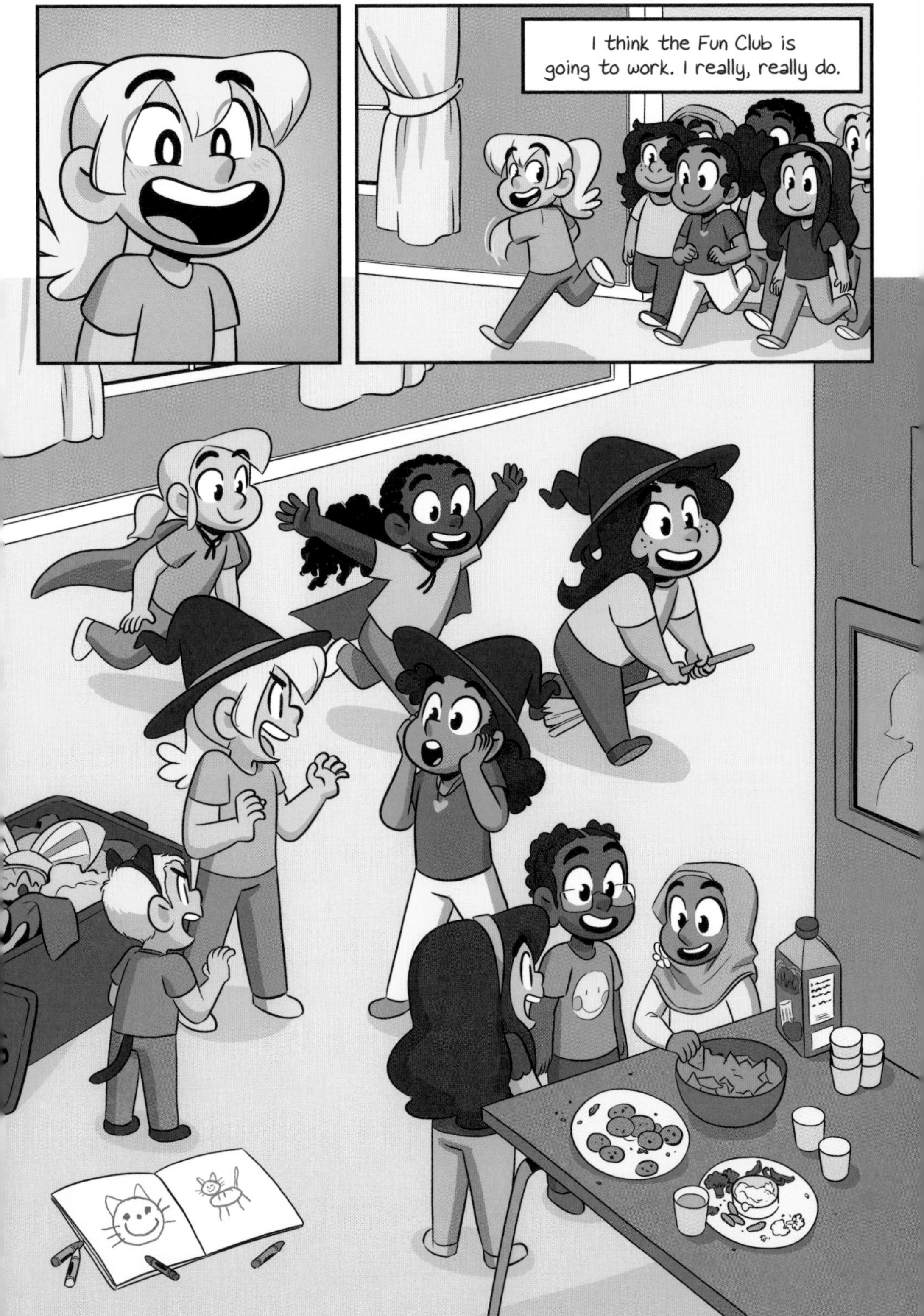
I think the Fun Club is going to work. I really, really do.

ANN M. MARTIN'S The Baby-sitters Club is one of the most popular series in the history of publishing — with more than 180 million books in print worldwide — and inspired a generation of young readers. Her novels include *Belle Teal*, *A Corner of the Universe* (a Newbery Honor book), *Here Today*, *A Dog's Life*, and *On Christmas Eve*, as well as the much-loved collaborations, *P.S. Longer Letter Later* and *Snail Mail No More*, with Paula Danziger, and *The Doll People* and *The Meanest Doll in the World*, written with Laura Godwin and illustrated by Brian Selznick. Ann lives in upstate New York.

KATY FARINA is the creator of the *New York Times* bestselling graphic novel adaptations of *Karen's Witch*, *Karen's Roller Skates*, and *Karen's Worst Day* by Ann M. Martin. She has painted backgrounds for *She-Ra and the Princesses of Power* at DreamWorks TV and has also done work for BOOM! Studios, Oni Press, and Z2 Comics. She lives in Los Angeles. Visit her online at katyfarina.com.

DON'T MISS THE OTHER BABY-SITTERS LITTLE SISTER GRAPHIC NOVELS!

A GRAPHIC NOVEL BY
KATY FARINA
BABY-SITTERS LITTLE SISTER
KAREN'S WITCH
BASED ON THE NOVEL BY
ANN M. MARTIN

A GRAPHIC NOVEL BY
KATY FARINA
BABY-SITTERS LITTLE SISTER
KAREN'S ROLLER SKATES
BASED ON THE NOVEL BY
ANN M. MARTIN

A GRAPHIC NOVEL BY
KATY FARINA
BABY-SITTERS LITTLE SISTER
KAREN'S WORST DAY
BASED ON THE NOVEL BY
ANN M. MARTIN

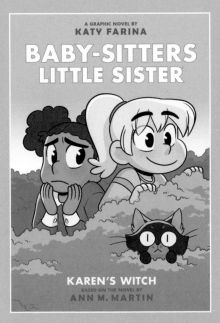